MW01488339

Becky Barker

Hanchart Land

Cerridwen Press

A Cerridwen Press Publication

www.cerridwenpress.com

Hanchart Land

ISBN 9781419956768
ALL RIGHTS RESERVED.
Hanchart Land Copyright © 2006 Becky Barker
Edited by Ann Leveille.
Cover art by Willo.

This book printed in the U.S.A. by Jasmine–Jade Enterprises, LLC.

Electronic book Publication July 2006
Trade paperback Publication September 2007

Cerridwen Press is an imprint of Ellora's Cave Publishing, Inc.®

Also by Becky Barker

ℬ

About the Author

❧

Becky Barker is a multi-published author whose steamy romance novels have been translated into more than a dozen foreign languages, into electronic format, and have been reissued in trade paperback as well as large print library editions.

Her personal hero is a former Marine who helped her create three pretty wonderful children. Rachel and her husband, Jerramy; Amanda and her husband, Jay; and Thad and his wife, Dara, all live within a few miles of Mom and Dad in rural Ohio.

Besides spending time with her family, Becky enjoys music, gardening, water sports and reading. She loves to hear from readers and can be reached through her website at BeckyBarker.com

Becky welcomes comments from readers. You can find her website and email address on her author bio page at www.cerridwenpress.com.

Tell Us What You Think
We appreciate hearing reader opinions about our books. You can email us at Comments@EllorasCave.com.

Hanchart Land

Dedication

&

This one's for my reading and writing friend, Julie Stroup, in thanks for her enthusiasm and support.

Trademarks Acknowledgement

&

The author acknowledges the trademarked status and trademark owners of the following wordmarks mentioned in this work of fiction:

Stetson: John B. Stetson Company

Chapter One

The thundering sound of a horse's hooves met Susan Hanchart's ears and her pulse lurched into the same thudding cadence. She locked the door of Shane's house for the final time, reminding herself to stay calm. She didn't have to look toward the fields to identify the lone rider approaching at such a breakneck speed. It had to be Luke Hanchart.

She'd known he would come and had dreaded this final confrontation. Turning on the porch, she moved toward the steps, stiffening her spine and squaring the weary droop of her shoulders. Every muscle and nerve in her body was strung painfully tight.

Luke reined his horse as he reached the grassy front yard and spotted her. His temper had been in a slow burn since he'd learned she was actually leaving. Hearing the news from someone outside the family had been bad enough, but seeing the rented moving van sent his temperature up another few notches.

He slowed his pace until he was within a few feet of the porch. The horse snorted from exertion and saddle leather creaked as man and beast shifted to stillness. Then Luke's gaze clashed with Susan's. Sparks flew along with the lid off his temper.

"What the hell do you think you're doing?" he demanded, anger and frustration evident in every hard line of his six-foot, two-hundred-pound body.

He knew exactly what she was doing, or he wouldn't have bothered to ride over here hell-for-leather, Susan thought to herself. Luke had been right there in the lawyer's office when Shane's will had been read. He knew his cousin had left his

11

share of the Hanchart land to her, his widow. With certain restrictions, of course. If Luke didn't like the way she had chosen to deal with those restrictions, there was nothing he could do about it now.

"I'm leaving today." Her calm response didn't give any indication of the sick dread she felt at having to move to the city.

She pulled her gaze from his and nodded toward the van that held all her worldly possessions. It had taken six months to get her affairs in order after Shane's death from a brain tumor at the age of twenty-five.

She had no regrets about leaving the house she'd shared with him for two painful years, but it was breaking her heart to leave the ranch and the way of life she treasured.

Luke's tone was grim. "I thought you weren't leaving for another two weeks."

"Sandy's daughter moved back earlier than expected, so she didn't need me anymore." Susan explained the premature loss of her job and only source of income.

He muttered another oath, his lean, hard face taking on an even tighter expression beneath the brim of his Stetson. "Matthews is saying you've agreed to sell to him. It better not be true," he insisted tersely.

Susan sighed. Even from the grave, Shane was twisting screws into her heart. He'd left the property to her along with a hefty mortgage and a mountain of debts. He'd known she'd have to sell, but his one stipulation was that she couldn't sell to his family.

The house, and several hundred acres of prime Hanchart property, was bordered by Luke's spread on the west and Raymond Matthews' property to the east. Both men wanted it.

She wished it could go back to the family, but her hands were legally tied. Shane's resentment of his cousin reached beyond death. Though she hated selling Hanchart land to an outsider, the bank and creditors had waited long enough for their money.

"You know I don't have any choice," she told him, her battle for composure making her sound cool and indifferent.

"The land's worth three times what he's offering," Luke insisted hotly.

"All I want is enough to pay off Shane's debts," she said.

"I'll pay off the damn debts and you can keep the property," he snapped. She'd rejected the same offer from his granddad, but he wasn't going to take no for an answer.

"I don't want loans or any more charity," she snapped right back at him. The decision was tough enough without having to repeatedly defend it to him.

"I'm not offering either," he bit out tersely. "I'd be paying you for the right to keep this land in the family. I'd pay a whole hell of a lot more and you know it. The deed will stay in your name, and you can live here as long as you want."

A shudder rippled down her spine. She couldn't tolerate living here one more day. The house was a constant reminder of her nightmarish marriage. She hated it. She wished she could sell it to Luke and be gone, but that wasn't an option.

"Even if the property stayed in my name, it would be totally unethical to let you pay Shane's debts."

He swore again. "When did it become unethical to pay a cousin's medical bills?"

If the debts had all been medical expenses, Susan might have accepted some help. She hadn't argued when Shane's grandfather, John Hanchart, had insisted on paying the funeral expenses. But the property had been mortgaged to pay off medical and gambling debts.

She didn't argue any further, just looked Luke straight in the eyes and shook her head negatively.

"Damn your stubborn hide," he said, seething.

For most of his life he'd had to fight off women who wanted him just for his money. Now when he badly wanted a woman to take advantage of his wealth, she flat-out refused.

He wondered if she was holding out for something beyond the payment of debts. "Have you signed a contract?"

"I haven't agreed to anything yet, but I have an appointment with an attorney tomorrow."

Her callous disregard for his heritage was unforgivable in his eyes. He loved the land with a passion few could understand. His roots were buried deep in Texas soil. The ranch was the foundation beneath his feet, the air he breathed, his heart and soul. Except for his granddad, nothing and no one else mattered more.

Luke considered himself the caretaker as his granddad had before him. He intended to pass it on to another generation intact. He wasn't about to let it go without a fight, but instinct warned him to back off and regroup.

"You were just going to drive away without so much as a word to anyone?"

The accusation stung even though she'd considered doing just that. "I was on my way to your place."

His steady glance encompassed the whole yard. "Where's your car?"

She'd sold it to finance the move to Houston, but pride kept her from admitting as much. Other than a few dollars for necessities, she was flat broke.

Her expression grew more obstinate, and he experienced a new wave of anger. "You sold it, too?"

She'd sold Shane's truck to help subsidize her small paycheck and make ends meet. In this land of vast spaces it had been a wrench to give up her car. But she'd had little choice.

"I won't need it in Houston. It's just an expensive liability."

She watched his big hands tighten on the reins, making the bay dance restlessly. He continued to glare at her. His anger and frustration were unnerving, yet she stood her ground with as much dignity as possible. The effort took its toll on her already strained emotions.

"I'll see you at the house."

The veiled threat was unsettling. Susan had clung to a very vague hope that he would understand and accept her decision. Obviously, she'd been wrong. She should have known he'd never accept the loss of any part of his beloved ranch.

Horse and rider whirled and headed back the way they'd come. She watched Luke's retreating figure with mixed emotions. He rode like a man born in the saddle, one with his horse, with an innate power and strength that few could emulate. He was a big, powerful man.

It would be easier to just leave without stopping at the main house, she mused. She was tempted, but didn't like taking the coward's path. She couldn't bring herself to leave without saying goodbye to John and the horses.

She would miss her hometown and the close-knit ranching community. More than that, she'd miss a way of life that was deeply ingrained in her nature. Although the move was the most logical solution to her employment and financial problems, she faced it with a heavy heart.

As she drove the rental van the few miles between Shane's house and Luke's, she mentally cataloged some of the things she would miss the most—endless blue skies that shimmered with sunlight, miles of pristine white fences and lush green pastures dotted with livestock. All the scents, sounds and sights of the countryside were burned into her memory.

This part of Texas was known for its sprawling ranches and the Hanchart property was no exception. The family owned over two thousand acres with several homesteads. Luke was an only child. He, as his father and grandfather before him, controlled the ranch and occupied the main house.

His cousins Shane, Brad and Linda had each been given smaller homesteads. Even though Susan had made her home on the property for the past two years, she'd always felt like an interloper in the family.

Because she'd never loved Shane, she'd never felt deserving of the affection, respect and loyalty that were a normal part of belonging.

The gates to the main entrance were an impressive wrought iron structure with a scrolled "H" on either side. More pristine white fences framed the half-mile paved driveway that led to the main house and barns.

Susan had always loved animals, especially horses. She'd spent a great deal of time these past few years tending to Luke's broodmares. The work with the livestock had been her salvation and saved her sanity on more than one occasion.

As usual, she skirted the Grecian-style two-story house and headed for the collection of barns near the rear of the property. There was no sign of Luke. For that she was thankful. She didn't know if she could withstand another round with him today. Her emotions never seemed to improve beyond constant turmoil.

One thing was certain. She needed to spend some time with the mares. Working with them was always soothing. At this point in her life they were her most cherished friends, the only beings she trusted with her heart.

Luke's two Border collies, Jack and Jill, raised a ruckus at the intrusion of the unfamiliar vehicle she was driving, but their defensive barks changed to welcoming yelps when they recognized her. She greeted them with words of praise and rubbed their silky heads, then continued toward the largest of the barns.

It took a minute for her eyes to adjust from bright sunshine to the more dimly lit building. The barn was swept clean, as always, and was in excellent repair. Everything on Luke's property was well maintained and Susan admired him for that. She hated to see livestock kept in unsanitary, unhealthy conditions.

When the horses heard her enter, their heads came popping over the half-doors of their stalls. An assortment of woofs and whinnies greeted her from eight compartments.

She started with the stall nearest the door and made her way along the row with quartered apples for each horse. After their treat and a loving caress, she bade them each a farewell in the soft, husky voice they knew and trusted.

"I promise not to forget you ladies, if you'll promise to take care of yourselves," she crooned softly.

The three-year-old chestnut in the last stall was the most difficult to leave. Susan had cared for Mariado since birth and had become particularly attached to the spirited filly. She was playful, friendly and could run like the wind. The two of them loved to race across the pastures.

"I hope you'll mind your manners once I've gone," she murmured, stroking the long, sleek mane and rubbing her cheek against the horse's neck. Almost overcome with emotion, she slid her arms around Mariado's head and hugged her tightly.

Luke had first introduced her to his horses after her parents were killed in a car accident. She'd needed to keep busy, and he'd told her to spend as much time with them as she liked. Her equine friends had become an outlet for so many turbulent emotions. That's why the loss of his most valued stallion had distressed her so much. He shared her love of animals and they both abhorred brutality against them. Yet it happened. The unending guilt squeezed her heart. If Luke ever learned her terrible secret, he'd despise her for it. She couldn't bear the thought.

When she'd married Shane and moved to Hanchart property, she'd continued to groom and exercise the horses, hoping to atone for some of the trouble she'd inadvertently caused. Since then all her spare time had been devoted to caring for his prized horses. It hurt to say goodbye knowing she'd never see them again.

"Maybe Luke will find someone else to race the wind with you," she told Mariado.

A deep baritone threaded with familiar, underlying anger, responded. "I've told you that you can keep the job, and the house. I'll pay you a decent wage to care for the horses."

Susan whirled to find Luke within touching distance, leaning against a wooden support beam near the stalls. His arms were crossed over his chest and his probing, silvery eyes were once again leveled at her. His tone was low and steady, but there was no doubting he was still very angry.

Caught up in her own misery, she hadn't heard him enter the building. She swiftly pulled her emotions under control. Dignity was about all she had left.

"You startled me."

It had been a long time since they'd been alone and this close. His six-foot frame seemed much taller than her own five-foot-two in such close proximity. With his broad chest and solidly muscled body, he radiated raw power and masculinity.

Dressed in worn jeans and a thin cotton shirt, he was male magnetism at its most devastating. Even though she considered herself immune to most men, her pulse always seemed to go into overdrive when he was near.

He didn't bother to apologize for startling her. He was a man totally at ease with his actions, the most self-assured man she'd ever known. He continued to level his steady gaze on her, causing all the little hairs on her body to tingle.

Susan was suddenly conscious of her own worn jeans and faded T-shirt, the dark circles under her eyes and less-than-flattering ponytail. None of it was especially different today, but his scrutiny was different. It made her more aware of other shortcomings.

Ever since the day she'd married Shane, Luke had kept his distance, both physically and emotionally. He hadn't said or done anything to change the status between them, yet a subtle change in the intensity of his regard made her more aware of him today.

Mentally chastising herself for such silly reactions, she drew in a deep breath of air to steady her riotous nerves and returned his bold regard.

"I sincerely appreciate the offer, but I still have to refuse."

He'd offered her a paying position with the broodmares when she'd first mentioned her plans to move to Houston. She'd refused because Shane had never been a husband in her heart. She didn't want favors from his family because she legally bore his name.

Now that the conditions of Shane's will presented more problems, it was even more tempting to accept Luke's offer. They both knew she'd hate living and working in the city yet some deep, inexplicable reluctance to be indebted to him kept her from taking the easy route and accepting. Besides that, her darkest secret was like a time bomb, at risk of exploding in her face.

Luke had accused her of being too stubborn and hardheaded, but she wasn't the only one. He apparently had no intention of accepting her decision. When he remained silent and brooding, she turned from him to stroke Mariado's head again.

"I was just saying my goodbyes," she explained, knowing he wouldn't ridicule her sentiment the way Shane had done so often. Luke was a breeder and horseman. He understood.

"Were you going to say goodbye to anyone else?" he asked. Before she could respond he shot another question at her. "How will you get by?"

Susan's pride had suffered some debilitating blows over the last four years, but she still had enough spirit to lift her chin and steadily return his gaze.

"The job in Houston pays well, and I'll be renting a room from a friend. I'll be fine."

His eyes probed more deeply. "You'll go back to school?"

She flinched at that. It seemed a lifetime ago that she'd gone off to college with youthful optimism and dreams of becoming a veterinarian. She'd had two carefree years of study before the loss of her parents had brought an abrupt end to college life.

She'd quit school, gotten a job and attempted to help Butch, her only sibling, through his last year of high school. Then he'd died too. College was just another sore subject between her and Luke.

"School doesn't fit into my plans," she said. It hadn't since the death of her youthful, carefree existence.

"Granddad's willing to set up a trust fund for your schooling. I'll pay Shane's debts and you can get on with your life. If it'll help salve your pride, you can sign a contract to come back here and work to repay the trust."

"Thanks, but no thanks," she said as politely but firmly as possible. At this point, college wasn't even a consideration. She couldn't imagine ever returning to an academic lifestyle.

When his eyes narrowed dangerously, she added, "John already took care of the funeral expenses. That was more than enough."

"There should have been a life insurance policy to protect your future. Granddad bought policies for all of us."

There had been, but Shane had borrowed from it to finance his gambling. It didn't matter because she wouldn't have taken a penny of his money except to pay his bills.

"I'm perfectly capable of taking care of myself," she told him. "Shane wasn't responsible for my welfare."

"He should have been."

It was another of the many ways Luke and his cousin had differed. Luke was proud, dependable and believed in old-fashioned values of a man taking full responsibility for the health and welfare of everyone in his family and employ.

Susan admired him for his belief, but she wouldn't allow him to shoulder what he believed was Shane's burden of responsibility.

"It's stupid for you to leave if you're not going back to school. You can work here, I'll take care of the damn debts and you can live at Shane's place for the rest of your life if you want."

"I can't stand to live there a minute longer," she said, a shudder accompanying the words.

His mouth tightened and his eyes grew even frostier. He hadn't considered the fact that she might still be grieving so much that she couldn't bear to stay in the house they'd shared.

"Hell."

Hell was an apt description of her state of mind. She knew Luke was misconstruing her reluctance. She wanted to scream with denial, but she needed to keep her emotions tightly in check.

Shane had insisted on a loving-couple charade in public, so people assumed they were madly in love. She'd never corrected that misconception, and trying to do so now would only complicate matters.

"Are you planning to wait tables in Houston?"

Besides her work with the mares, for which she refused even a penny of compensation, Susan had taken an evening job as a waitress in a small local diner. She knew the Hancharts had considered it a slap in the face, a deliberate attempt to humiliate the family, but she hadn't meant it that way.

"There's nothing wrong with waitress work," she grumbled. "I didn't find it demeaning in any way, and I was glad to have the work. I'm sorry if my job offended the family, but there aren't that many options in Monroe."

Luke couldn't argue with facts and didn't try. "So you will be doing waitress work?"

"No. I've accepted a job as a bank teller."

His eyes flashed, and her stance and tone became defensive. "There's not a damned thing wrong with being a bank teller, either."

"Not if you like it," he snapped. "But you hate being shut indoors all day and you know it. You're a natural with the livestock. That's the sort of job you should be looking for."

"Well, there aren't a lot of high-paying jobs available for someone without a degree or specialized training. I was happy to get the bank job."

Mariado whinnied and nudged Susan for attention. She automatically lifted a hand to stroke the mare's jaw.

"I have an alternative," he declared, his expression stony and cold. "We could get married."

She turned and stared at him, her big blue eyes going wide with astonishment. She had to have heard him wrong.

"What?"

Luke's mouth tightened briefly. He couldn't tell if she was genuinely shocked or just playing innocent. She wouldn't be the first woman who'd tried to manipulate him into matrimony. She might be the first who had a chance at succeeding.

"I said, marry me and stay on the ranch," he repeated, mobilizing himself with languid grace to diminish the few feet between them.

The words weren't any less enervating with repetition. It was hard to know if her sudden breathlessness was due to his shocking proposal or the equally disturbing nearness of his big body. He'd moved so close that she had to tilt her head slightly to retain eye contact.

"You can't be serious, so how do you expect me to respond?" Susan wondered aloud.

His reply was terse. "I'm serious as hell. If you aren't going back to school, there's no reason not to remarry. I'll give you a cash settlement to pay off Shane's debts and the property stays in the family. You won't have to move to the city and you can decide if, when and where you want to work."

Susan's eyes went wider. She'd known Luke would do almost anything to keep her from selling Hanchart land, but she'd never thought he'd resort to a marriage proposal.

Her gaze locked with his, curious and searching. She doubted if he had any tender feelings for her other than a familial responsibility. He might consider her a valuable live-stock handler but he certainly didn't love her.

Sometimes he was so grim and cold that she wondered if he hated her. The two of them had been an item for a brief time, and he'd been furious when she'd married Shane. He'd seemed detached and unforgiving ever since.

For the most part, he'd kept his distance, but she couldn't really blame him for that. Her marriage to his cousin had been a cruel affair all around. The determined glint in his eyes made it clear that this was no joking matter to him.

"You're talking about a marriage of convenience? The property reverts back to the family through marriage and I'm free to live and work here the rest of my life?" Despite a multitude of misgivings, the idea actually appealed--until he expanded on it.

"I'm not offering a marriage in name only," he ground out, irritated by her small spurt of interest in a platonic relationship. "I want a family, and I don't plan on fathering any bastards. If we get married it'll be a real marriage."

Susan continued to stare at him, dumbfounded. Her tired brain could hardly comprehend this latest offer.

"We're not even romantically involved."

"I'm not looking for romance, and I doubt you are either. I'm talking about an equally beneficial partnership, a com-mitment for the future and eventually a family of our own."

Susan lowered her lashes so that he wouldn't see how deeply those words touched her. Since losing her family, she'd been so alone and bereft. She felt as though her feet were rooted in constantly shifting sands and battled with desolation every day.

She kept one hand on Mariado's mane and leaned against the stall door for support. His words had a dizzying effect. She hadn't told anyone about her fierce desire for children, for a family to love and care for, someone to love her. Luke seemed to have reached into her soul and touched on the one area that could gain him leverage.

His proposal made her wonder if he might have similar desires. Was he ever so lonely he thought he'd die? Did he ever yearn for a family? He'd lost his parents at an early age and the grandmother who'd raised him had passed away the year before her parents.

She'd thought her dreams of babies and a real family were doomed, yet he made her realize just how much they still meant to her. He was tempting her with a brass ring she desperately wanted, but had thought out of reach.

"You want children?" she managed to ask, lifting curious eyes to read his reaction to her question.

For just an instant the question caused his control to slip. She caught a rare glimpse of unguarded emotion. What she saw, the hunger and need, was nearly her undoing. A tremor shook her.

"I'd like a dozen," he assured her, tone curt. "But I'd settle for one or two."

Her eyes widened even further. There was nothing she'd like more than to have a big, boisterous, loving family. The sudden mental image of little boys with sand-colored hair and devilish gray eyes made her heart thud in a painful rhythm.

She quickly regained control of her wayward imagination. She was nobody's fool, and she knew there was more to a family than just having lots of offspring. There had to be more to Luke's proposal.

"What makes you think we could possibly make it work?" she asked.

"You're not squeamish about pregnancy and birth. You've proven that with the horses. As far as I know you're strong and healthy, intelligent and attractive," he explained as though listing one of his mare's bloodlines.

"So I'll not only bring a dowry of property, but you think I'll make a good broodmare?" she asked in amazement, glancing down the row of horses in their stalls. She didn't know whether to feel honored or insulted. "I hope you don't think I'll be just one of many," she grumbled in annoyance.

She couldn't have cared less about Shane's infidelities, but she instinctively recoiled at the thought of Luke with other women. She wasn't about to become a broodmare for a roving stallion.

Her breath shattered and her thoughts scattered when his lips curved in a mocking smile. It staggered her. Gone were thoughts of infidelity as she found herself wondering what it would be like to once again coax a real smile or laughter from this taciturn man.

"I swear I don't see myself as stud material," he assured her derisively. "If I wanted a harem I'd have started it a long time ago. I think we both want the same things when it comes to a family."

"Like what?"

"Like commitment, loyalty, a solid foundation and kids who'll love our way of life as much as we do."

Her breath caught painfully in her chest. She couldn't help but agree with him. Those were the most important things she'd lost along with her family. If she ever regained them, she would cherish them always.

"You're really serious about marriage?"

"Why not? I'm thirty years old, and I haven't found the proverbial perfect woman yet so…"

Susan cut him off sharply. "So you'll settle for an imperfect one?" she snapped, hurt and angered by the pain.

Luke's eyes flashed and his jaw clenched, but he continued in a steady tone. "So, I'll settle for a dependable mate who isn't a society nitwit only interested in money and social standing."

His explanation soothed her temper somewhat. She didn't like the idea of being someone he would settle for if he couldn't find anyone better, but she did empathize with him about the social pressures.

It was easy to understand his distaste for the women who'd thrown themselves at him over the years because of his wealth and social status. She'd seen more than her share of scheming mothers with pushy daughters vying for the Hanchart name and money.

There had been plenty of normal, sincere women too. She knew he'd had lovers and women who truly cared about him. Shane had delighted in telling her about Luke's women. But as far as she knew, he'd never proposed marriage to anyone.

The proposal was tempting until Susan gave it a little more thought and considered the physical side of the matter. Her relationship with Shane had been platonic for the most part. After one nightmare of a night when he'd forced himself on her, she couldn't imagine intimacy with any man. She desperately wanted children, but she wasn't sure she had the courage to conceive them.

A blush stole up her cheeks as another thought came to mind. "I hope you aren't another one of those men who think it their duty to service a sexually deprived widow," she asked, half angry, half embarrassed.

Luke's gaze sharpened. He was close enough that she could feel the increased tension in his body. He grabbed her elbow and turned her more fully toward him.

"No, I'm not," he snapped. "Who's been bothering you?"

Susan wasn't about to tell him that a couple of Shane's so-called friends had paid her visits to offer themselves for pleasure. She'd been confused at first, then stunned and furious.

"It wasn't anything I couldn't handle," she assured. She'd used a shotgun to run off one particularly persistent vulture when her verbal refusals hadn't been sufficient.

"Have you been feeling deprived?"

The question brought a wash of hot color to her face. "No," she snapped.

Luke studied her flushed cheeks. He didn't understand her embarrassment or the flare of temper. She wasn't an innocent, so the question shouldn't have flustered her so much. Still, the touch of color to her deathly pale cheeks was a vast improvement.

"Are you afraid of intimacy with me?" His voice was suddenly low and intense.

Susan was taken aback by the question. Shane had often taunted her with details of Luke's exploits with women. He'd labeled his virile cousin as "rough and ready", but she hadn't believed much that he said.

Luke might not have any trouble verbalizing the question, but she had trouble answering it. The history of their personal relationship was complex.

He'd been especially kind to her after her parents' deaths. They'd shared a few dates, and she'd woven a few romantic dreams around him. Their relationship hadn't developed very far, but there had been some strong chemistry between them.

Shane had recognized the mutual interest and set about putting a stop to it. Within weeks he'd blackmailed her into marriage, and she'd been too overwhelmed by her own problems to worry about Luke's feelings. She'd been thankful that he'd kept his distance these past two years because she always felt a jumble of conflicting emotions when he was near.

"Susan?" he prompted her out of her reverie. "Are you afraid of me?"

Her eyes widened and met his. Even though he had a reputation for having a quick temper and of being ruthless at times, she'd never feared him. How could you be afraid of a man who crooned to baby animals, had a gentle touch with all his livestock and a caring attitude about everything and everyone around him?

"I'm not afraid of you," she finally managed. Wary, yes. Shane had made her wary of all men, but she wasn't afraid. "I'm just finding it hard to take it all in. Why are you so certain we could make it work?"

Chapter Two

৪৩

Instead of offering her more explanations, Luke reached out and pulled her into his arms, his eyes never leaving the ever-widening brilliance of hers.

Susan flattened her hands on his chest and tilted her head toward him with a gasp of surprise on her lips. Then he took her mouth with his own. He was neither rough nor particularly gentle, but he kissed her with the strength and sureness of a man who knew what he wanted. He tasted like morning coffee, a little tart, a little sweet, and kicked her adrenaline into overdrive more swiftly than caffeine.

She was stiff and unresponsive at first while her mind and body dealt with the shock of being so close to him, actually touching him for the first time in years. He was furnace hot, rock solid and pure male.

It had been a long time since she'd been kissed, really kissed by someone intent on giving and taking pleasure. She wouldn't have expected to enjoy being so close to any man, but the scent, feel and taste of him was unique.

His mouth was firm but surprisingly warm and tantalizing. His scent was a mixture of fresh air and pure male. His hands on her waist were hot and huge, nearly spanning it, but his grip wasn't too tight or forceful.

She'd kissed her share of men, yet she'd never enjoyed kissing anyone as much as Luke. For years now, forgetting the impact of his kisses had been a necessity of survival, but this reminder sent a flood of reaction washing over her.

Susan found herself slowly relaxing and enjoying the embrace. Her lips softened to better fit his and responded with growing fervor. His tongue sought and gained entrance into her mouth and then everything changed with a fierce rush of long-denied passion.

Her body became more pliable as she molded herself closer to him. She slid her arms over his shoulders and then wrapped them about his neck. He drew her more firmly against his hard body, so tight that she could feel the growing evidence of his arousal.

A small gasp escaped her when he slowly ground his hips against her abdomen. Something deep within her went liquid in response. She sank the fingers of one hand into the thickness of his hair and clung to his head, demanding more.

When his tongue had completed a thorough exploration of her mouth, she stroked hers against it, and felt a shudder ripple over his body, fusing them even closer.

He continued to plunder her mouth while he eased her back against the wooden door of the stall. Then he held her captive with the strength of his hips while one of his hands slid beneath the hem of her shirt.

A low moan escaped Susan as his long, strong fingers sought and cupped her right breast. Currents of hot electricity coursed through her, leaving her quaking in the wake. Combined moans of pleasure swirled in their mouths as his thumb stroked one nipple into pebbled hardness and then shifted to give the other nipple equal attention.

Susan trembled and her knees grew weak. She grasped two handfuls of hair and clung to the thick mass while her mouth grew more insistent against his. Their kisses became deeper and longer and more intoxicating.

Luke slid a hand up her back and unclipped her bra. Then he was lifting her shirt high enough to enable him to caress both bared breasts with his big, calloused hands.

She was coming apart at the seams. They'd done some petting in the past, but he'd had never taken such liberties, never made her burn so high so fast. Her hands clutched his head, drawing him closer while arching her back to give him more freedom. She was stunned by the violence of her own responses, yet unwilling to stop the onslaught.

The low, primitive groans being drawn from deep in Luke's chest assured her that he was equally affected. Maybe it was just a man's reaction to a woman, two mature adults starving for human contact, but she was beyond caring.

Their kisses became more inflamed and their breathing more erratic. Susan felt the heavy thud of his heart and the throbbing thrust of his arousal. His fingers stroked and plucked at her nipples, making her wild with need. Her legs quivered until she was afraid they would crumple beneath her.

Luke solved the problem by thrusting a hard, jean-clad thigh between her legs and shifting it tightly into the cradle of her thighs to support her weight. Then he dragged his mouth from hers and pierced her with a searing gaze.

"I have to taste the rest of you," he insisted, his tone savage.

Before she could catch her breath or respond, he was simultaneously lifting her and dipping his head under her shirt. At the first touch of his lips on her breast she nearly went wild, clawing at his shoulders, twisting and turning in reaction to the sweet torture.

"Luke!" She cried out with the sheer intensity of desire created by the sucking pressure he applied to first one nipple and then the other. Her breasts were sensitive, but she'd never felt a man's greedy mouth on that sensitive flesh. The reality of it was stunning.

"Luke!" She managed to whisper a strangled cry.

"Our babies would find nourishment here and so would their daddy," he told her, his tone deep and heavy with arousal as he continued to suckle at her breasts.

His words shot more heat through her limbs. She felt the emptiness of her womb and craved a fulfillment she'd never known. Her body actually ached with wanting.

There had always been an element of primitive excitement when Luke was near, but it had been carefully reined. She'd never realized how explosive the passion could be. Grasping his head, she dragged his mouth back to hers for longer, deeper, hotter kisses.

Their bodies strained closer, stroking each other from thigh to chest until they were oblivious of everything else. Heat built to incinerating levels until Mariado, offended by lack of attention, butted them strongly with her head. Their precarious balance was threatened.

He reacted swiftly, steadying her while watching her with eyes that devoured her features until she felt raw and exposed. His voice was hoarse when he spoke.

"We'd better put an end to this right now," he insisted, eyes burning like hot steel. He sucked in a deep breath before continuing. "I could take you standing up right here," he insisted tersely. "And the hell with privacy."

His gruff words made Susan's stomach muscles clench and her breasts swell with heaviness. She knew that he was an extremely private person. So was she, but she'd been equally affected by their embrace.

It shocked her to realize how passionate she felt in his arms. Her body's reactions were more fierce than anything she'd ever known. It was a little frightening, and her first instinct was to completely withdraw from his embrace.

"You shouldn't be so shocked," he told her, continuing to support most of her weight. "I've always known the passion between us would be explosive."

Susan hadn't known, nor had any idea. She wasn't sure she liked the wild feelings he aroused, but it was a relief to learn that Shane hadn't destroyed her ability to respond to a man.

Still, she was shaken and trembling. She made a determined effort to steady herself on her own two legs and regulate her erratic breathing. He helped right her clothing with so much ease that she felt no embarrassment.

Then Luke allowed her to put a small distance between them, but his gaze boldly announced that she couldn't escape what was between them.

"You can run, but you can't hide," he warned. "You might not want involvement, but I think we just proved you're not indifferent to me."

Susan was having a difficult time calming her riotous emotions. She was amazed at how much pleasure she'd found in his arms and the inordinate amount of pleasure he seemed to derive from her responses.

Was she really a wanton widow? No. With a mental shake of her head she conceded the idiocy of that thought. She'd certainly never known the kind of passion he'd just stirred in her. Still, she wondered if he thought her wanton, believed that she was a widow in need of a man. The thought heated her already over-warm flesh.

"You think the physical attraction is enough to sustain a marriage?"

"Not even close," he returned bluntly. "But it's a damned good start. Granddad says the chemistry jump-starts a marriage, then the man and wife have to work their butts off to make a lasting commitment. I'd say we have all the sparks for a good jump-start."

The heat in her face never had a chance to recede. He kept her so completely off balance. But the mention of the Hanchart patriarch had her frowning. John and his wife Alma had raised Luke after their son died at an early age. John had long since given the reins of the ranch over to Luke, but he was still active and verbal about what he liked and didn't like.

"Did John have anything to do with your marriage proposal?" she asked, holding his gaze with difficulty.

"Not hardly," Luke drawled. "He's been nagging me for ten years to get married and give him great-grandbabies, but no more now than usual."

"He and everyone else in this area would have a field day with a marriage between us," she warned.

Was the flicker of tension in his eyes annoyance, or satisfaction that she was obviously taking his proposal seriously?

"I don't give a damn what anybody else thinks," he stated succinctly.

Susan didn't think he cared much about his local popularity. She searched his features to see if there were any telltale signs of concern.

"People can be cruel."

Neither of them elaborated, but they both knew people would criticize her for marrying so soon after Shane's death. They'd call Luke a lecher and accuse him of preying on her vulnerability.

Some would call her a slut and a gold-digger. There would be no secret about marrying to keep the family's land holdings intact. Nothing was ever really private in so small a community.

The Hanchart money and power would prevent them from becoming social outcasts, but things could get very unpleasant. The rest of the Hanchart family might be the worst offenders.

Susan would prefer to isolate herself on the ranch and ignore popular opinions, but she knew that was nearly impossible.

"I can handle it," Luke assured her. "Can you?"

She gave him a sad smile. "Talk is cheap. There was a time when it would have bothered me a lot." That was when her parents were living and her family had been a pillar of the community, before her life had been shattered into a million pieces. "Very little bothers me now."

His eyes were glittering slits of silver as they scoured her face for signs of emotions in conflict with her words. "Does that mean you're accepting my proposal?"

A frown creased her brow. "It means I'll give it some thought."

His reaction was swift and harsh. "I thought you couldn't afford to wait any longer. It's stupid to move everything to Houston if we're going to be married. You can move in right now."

Susan was a little taken aback by his attitude. She knew there was a strong physical attraction between them, but there had to be more to his impatience. Even though she understood how important the land was to him she couldn't help resenting his impatience to have his way.

"That would really stir up the gossip," she insisted.

"You could go back to Shane's place."

"No!" She was equally adamant about that.

"Then stay here. Juan and Rosa can move into the house as chaperons or Granddad can move back for a while if you think it's necessary."

Juan and Rosa Lopez were part of the ranch staff, he a foreman and she a housekeeper. They had their own smaller house, as did John, but everyone occasionally stayed at the main house.

"I'm not worried about chaperons." She might be a little wary of being alone with him, but not enough to suffer several unfamiliar companions.

"Good, because I'm not too fond of having a house full of people, either."

Susan absently stroked Mariado's neck while she gave more thought to Luke's suggestion, trying to study it from every conceivable angle. It would solve a lot of her immediate problems. She wouldn't have to move to the city, leave her beloved horses or worry about her dismal finances.

On the other hand, her experience with marriage had been terrible. The brutal death of her youthful dreams had convinced her there were no Prince Charmings. She never wanted to be trapped in a bad marriage again, but how was one to know? There were no assurances. Would it be wiser to marry for strictly practical reasons? Was it so wrong to yearn for security and the promise of a family?

She liked what she knew about Luke. Without Shane's interference, their relationship might have developed into a deeper commitment. They shared a solid foundation of growing up in the same community with a long line of Texas blood in their veins.

They seemed to want the same things from life—home, family and commitment. At least she thought they did.

"I've learned there aren't any guarantees in life. What if we can't make it work?"

"We make it work," he insisted tersely. "If we get married, it's for life. That's the only string attached. If you marry me, I'll never agree to a divorce. Never. So understand that from the start."

"Never's a long time if we learn to hate each other," she felt compelled to mention.

"I swear on my life that I'll never abuse you or cheat on you. I'll expect the same vow of fidelity, regardless of how tough things get. Other than that, there are no strings."

"Not even a prenuptial agreement?"

Luke's frown deepened. Was she testing him? "Do you think either one of our mothers signed one?"

That brought a small smile to her lips. Her parents had been deeply in love. Regardless of everything that had come since their deaths, Susan would always be grateful for the emotional security their love had instilled in her.

"Are you hesitating because you're still in mourning for Shane?"

Her brow furrowed. Shane might be dead, but the knowledge he'd used to blackmail her would always be a threat to her peace of mind. If she married Luke, it could possibly destroy any hope for their happiness.

"So what's your answer?" he demanded impatiently. "Can you walk away or will you stay and marry me?"

His expression and tone were so fierce that it made Susan wonder if he resented the attraction they shared.

"I have to ask just one more question," she insisted, her eyes locking with his.

"I understand that the land is important to you, but does your sudden proposal have anything at all to do with Shane?" She didn't want a marriage based on misplaced loyalty, a sense of responsibility or even male rivalry. Luke hesitated just an instant longer than she could tolerate. She stiffened and moved abruptly away from him. "Then it's thanks, but no thanks." Turning, she headed for the door. "I have to be on my way."

"Dammit, Susan, wait," he commanded sharply.

She ignored him and hurried toward the door, but the instant she stepped out of the barn and into the blistering sunshine her head started to whirl. The midmorning temperature was already in the nineties and hit her like a ball of fire. First she was stunned, then everything went dark. It was like falling in slow motion and being helpless to stop.

Luke was close enough to catch her and break her fall. He scooped her into his arms, realizing that she'd passed out. He held her close to his chest while striding toward the house and yelling for the housekeeper.

"Rosa!" His voice had a resounding roar that easily carried across the barnyard to the house.

The short, round Hispanic woman met him at the back door, her dark eyes concerned. She held the door while he carried Susan into the house.

"What happened?"

"I don't know. She just rushed out of the barn and collapsed. It might be the heat."

"She's used to the heat," Rosa argued. "She's probably collapsed from exhaustion. Put her on the couch in the living room. I'll get some water and a damp cloth for her forehead."

"Call Doc Peters and see if he can get out here or if I should bring her to the clinic."

Rosa went to do his bidding while Luke eased Susan onto the sofa. He shoved aside cushions so that she could lie flat, laid her arms next to her body and then tugged her boots off her feet to make her more comfortable.

When he reached to brush a wayward strand of hair from her face, her eyelids fluttered and she began to stir.

"Susan?"

A frown creased her forehead and she slowly opened her eyes, staring at his face in confusion. She lifted a hand to brush her fingers over her eyes then gradually became more aware of her surroundings. It was unsettling to find herself in the house and not remember getting there. Lying on the sofa with Luke leaning over her did nothing to reassure her.

"What happened?" she managed to ask, her voice a bare whisper. She tried to lift herself on one elbow but found the effort too much for her.

His jaw clenched. "I don't know what happened. You just fainted."

"I've never fainted in my life."

She'd had a lot of shocks in her twenty-four years, but she'd never fainted from them. She certainly wasn't fragile and didn't like the thought of being helpless or at anyone's mercy.

"There's a first time for everything," he countered. "And you were definitely out cold."

Susan's frown deepened. She might have passed out, but every cell in her body was still functioning properly. She knew because they were reacting to his nearness again.

Then Rosa entered the room chattering a mile a minute. Luke straightened and stepped aside while the housekeeper clucked over their patient.

"Here, honey, take a long drink of water and then we'll cool you down a little until the doctor gets here."

She eased a hand under Susan's shoulder and lifted her a little so that she could drink. "You probably got a little dehydrated. I got a hold of the doctor on his mobile phone. He's close by, so he agreed to come right over. You just need to rest until he gets here."

"I don't need a doctor," Susan said after drinking thirstily. She didn't want to hurt anyone's feelings, but her strength was returning, and she didn't have money for house calls. "I'm feeling much better already."

"Then you'll be able to tell Doc Peters exactly what's wrong," said Luke. He settled himself into a nearby chair and kept his steady gaze leveled on her.

Susan's gaze flew to his. "I was just temporarily overcome by the heat," she insisted.

"Maybe," he drawled, "but we'll let the doc decide."

Rosa gently nudged her to lie flat and placed a cool compress on her forehead.

"I'll get you some more water. That must have tasted pretty good."

As soon as Rosa out of the room, she held the cloth to her head and pulled herself into a sitting position. It alarmed her that the action made her dizzy again.

"Not quite ready for the races?" Luke asked in a derisive tone.

She frowned and her eyes shot sparks at him. She hated feeling so weak and wimpy. "It was probably delayed shock from your proposal," she accused, needing an outlet for her frustration. She also hated being such a jumble of nerves and conflicting emotions.

"Anything that affects you so strongly should be taken more seriously, shouldn't it?"

"I was taking it very seriously," she explained, "until you all but admitted that the offer was some sort of misguided attempt to make up for all the wrongs Shane ever did."

Luke's features hardened and his hands clenched into fists at his sides. "If you hadn't run out of the barn in such a huff, I'd have explained. I only hesitated because I couldn't find any diplomatic way to say I never want to hear his name mentioned between us again."

Some of the tension drained from her at his heated declaration. She didn't doubt his sincerity. She'd be happy to forget Shane ever existed too, and might consider Luke's proposal if it had nothing to do with her dead husband.

"Is that the absolute truth?" she asked, her expression tight.

He didn't seem too pleased with the question, but he responded without hesitation, "I don't lie."

It was a simple declaration, but incredibly important to her. She'd been raised to believe that honesty was the best policy, that lies and deceit were unacceptable. But Shane had thrived on deceiving people. It had shaken her faith in herself and humanity.

Could Luke restore that faith? More importantly, could she marry him without being completely honest about her sham of a marriage? Could they really dismiss Shane from their lives and make a better future for themselves?

"If we were to marry, do you really think we could put the past behind us? Bury it forever and start fresh?"

"There'll be plenty of people willing to remind us on a regular basis," he assured grimly, "but we can do anything we set our minds to."

"You can honestly forget that I was married to your cousin?"

His face tightened into even more uncompromising lines, but she didn't know if it was due to the mention of her marriage or his inability to forgive and forget. The roar of a truck in the drive distracted him, so he rose to go to the window.

"Doc Peters is here. He must have been really close or he broke a few speed limits. I think he has a soft spot for you, anyway."

Susan had a soft spot for the doctor too. He was well loved in this area. The accident that had killed her dad had left her mother in a coma for weeks before death. She'd never regained consciousness. Doc Peters had lent a faithful shoulder during her hospitalization. He hadn't charged a penny for his frequent visits.

"I can't afford to pay him, and I don't like accepting charity," she said.

Luke turned a cool gaze back to her. "You were here caring for my horses. I'll see that he's paid."

Her expression made it clear that she didn't like accepting anything from him either, which made his expression even more fierce.

"It's not charity, you hardheaded little idiot."

Susan didn't respond even though her glare told him what she thought of his generosity and his insults. No one could accuse Luke Hanchart of being a smooth talker. Though his arrogance annoyed her, it was a welcome relief from Shane's glib ways.

Rosa and Doctor Peters entered the room together and put an end to the discussion. The housekeeper gave her more water while the doctor pulled out a blood pressure cuff.

He was a tall, thin, balding man with a deeply lined face that showed years of work and worry. Susan didn't know how old he was. She assumed he was in his seventies, but she knew he wouldn't retire until he died. Despite his advancing years, his eyes were bright with intelligence and his mind was still sharp.

"Well, young lady, what have you been doing with yourself?" he asked.

As the county's only general practitioner, he'd helped bring most of the local population into the world. She was no exception.

"I don't know. I was just leaving the barn and the heat seemed to hit me with more force than usual."

Peters nodded and stuck a thermometer in her mouth while he checked her pressure. He took her pulse and then started to scold.

"I suppose you've been keeping some pretty long hours, not sleeping or eating properly and fretting about this big move. Right?"

She had no chance to respond before he continued.

"I told you to slow down and take care of yourself, but nobody ever listens to the old doctor. Everybody thinks they're superhuman these days. You just push your bodies to the very limit and then call me when you collapse. Didn't I warn you to slow down and take better care of yourself?"

"Yes," she mumbled around the thermometer.

"And did you take my advice?"

"No," she mumbled again.

"You need a few days of complete rest. A couple weeks wouldn't hurt. I can give you a complete physical, but there's nothing wrong that some common sense couldn't cure. You've just pushed too hard this time."

"I've never fainted before."

"It's your body's way of warning you to slow down. It'd be wise to heed the warning."

It was easy for him to tell her what she needed, but not so easy for her to accomplish. She didn't have the luxury of taking a few weeks to regain her usual strength. She was just about to tell him that she needed to be on the road by evening when Luke intervened.

"Susan and I are going to be married soon," he stunned them all by announcing. His expression told her he was taking the decision out of her hands and if she had any remaining doubts, she should air them now.

A few tense seconds passed. When she didn't contradict him, he continued, "She was planning to stay in Houston with some friends until the arrangements are made, but if she needs rest, she can stay here. Rosa will spoil her, and I'll make sure she doesn't overexert herself."

Rosa was clapping her hands in delight. "Married! Oh! You're going to be married. I'm so happy for you! I'll make a cake and we'll have a celebration. I love weddings."

Doctor Peters was looking from one to the other. His shrewd eyes didn't miss much, but all he saw was an unspoken understanding between them.

"I'll add my congratulations. It sounds like a good match to me. You two can come in to the clinic on Monday and get the blood work done. I'll examine Susan a little more thoroughly then. She may need a vitamin supplement, but I think she just needs to slow down for a little while."

"Sounds good, Doc. We'll be there early Monday. I appreciate your coming today."

The doctor shrugged aside the words of thanks. He was already repacking his bag and preparing to leave. Luke offered him lunch but he declined. It was Saturday, he had a fishing trip planned and was anxious to be on his way.

Susan added her thanks and the men headed outside together. She accepted a big hug from Rosa, but she was still feeling a little disoriented and bemused by the sudden turn of events. Apparently she'd just accepted Luke's proposal. Acceptance by lack of rejection, to be exact. She could only pray it wasn't the biggest mistake of her life.

He didn't love her. Once upon a time she'd been half in love with him, but she wasn't the same person now. Too much had happened in the intervening time. She couldn't give her heart too freely or completely because it was severely damaged. She needed firm control of her emotions. Any more trauma and she might not survive.

They might still be fascinated with each other, but all they seemed to have going for them was physical attraction and a desire for a family. Maybe, just maybe, it could be expanded to a really caring relationship.

Chapter Three

Luke had ordered her to take it easy. Susan didn't want to blindly obey him, yet she wasn't feeling strong enough to protest. Sheer exhaustion kept her submissive. He asked what boxes or bags she needed from the rental truck and carried the necessities to a room Rosa kept prepared for guests.

After a short discussion regarding her intention of staying and giving their relationship a chance, they'd agreed to store her small collection of furniture and family keepsakes in another spare bedroom.

One of his ranch hands was ordered to return the truck to the rental agency. Susan watched it leave the property with a sense of having burned her bridges. She called her friend Lora and told her she'd changed her mind about coming to Houston.

Lora had wished her luck, but thankfully hadn't asked a lot of questions. She accepted her decision, wished her well and told her the offer was open-ended.

Luke warned her that he expected her to follow the doctor's orders and relax. He didn't want her working with the horses or doing anything more strenuous than unpacking some suitcases.

She didn't have the strength to disobey those orders, either, but she wasn't used to having idle time on her hands. The last few years had been spent in a frenzied attempt to stay too busy to think.

Over the next couple hours, she spent time moving into her room and reacquainting herself with Luke's home. The room she'd been given was one of six huge bedrooms with adjoining baths on the second floor. It was brightly lit with two long windows that faced the east and offered the morning sun. Sheer lacy curtains gently fluttered in the breeze.

Decorated in shades of cream and mauve with plush carpeting and mahogany furnishings, the room was both elegant and comfortable. Besides a big closet that swallowed her wardrobe, there was a chest of drawers and a dressing table with mirror that glistened from Rosa's attention.

The downstairs was also homey and welcoming with some elegant rooms and some very comfortable ones. She'd paid several visits here and was familiar with the layout, but enjoyed exploring more thoroughly.

A wide hallway with a winding staircase divided the house. On one side was a formal dining room and living room for entertaining large numbers of people. The other side had a small ranch office and a huge family room.

The big yellow and white kitchen was at the back of the house and stretched the entire length of the building. It had a breakfast nook big enough to seat eight people and expanded to seat more, if necessary.

Luke had grabbed a couple sandwiches and headed back out to work, but Rosa and Susan shared a more leisurely lunch. The housekeeper was at least twenty years her senior with a maternal streak a mile long. She was good company and a great cook.

Susan was surprised that she didn't mention the upcoming nuptials, but assumed Luke had something to do with that. He'd probably warned Rosa to go slow with the plans.

Her own five children were grown and married, but she was notorious for adopting strays like Susan. Although they'd never spent much time together, they respected each other and had become casual friends.

Rosa refused to let her help clean the kitchen or do any household chores. Within a few of hours after her fainting spell, she was feeling truly restless and bored.

"How about some television?" the housekeeper suggested, realizing their guest needed to be busy. "Or there's a bunch of videos."

Susan smiled her thanks, but she didn't care much for television. Videos didn't appeal, nor did reading at the moment. She wanted to ride, but knew she shouldn't do that.

"Could you sleep for a while?" asked Rosa. "Nobody will care if you take a nap."

"I'm not really sleepy, and I'm not used to napping in the daytime."

"Why don't you put on a bikini and go soak up some sun. There's a wonderful swimming pool out back that doesn't get nearly enough use. John comes around nearly every day for a little exercise and Luke likes to swim, but neither of them spend much time out there. It's such a waste."

The idea sounded close to heaven. Susan loved the water, but she hadn't been near a pool since college. Unfortunately, she didn't own a decent bathing suit.

"It will be wonderful therapy," added Rosa. "I have a whole collection of suits in all sizes for when we have visitors. They're stored in the pantry. Come and see."

Susan followed her to a small room off the west side of the kitchen. They sorted through stacks of bathing suits until they found a one-piece blue maillot that looked like it might fit her.

"You shouldn't be running up and down the stairs," said Rosa, pointing to their right. "Just use the washroom through this door to try it."

She indicated a small half-bath that adjoined the pantry and laundry room. Susan stepped inside and closed the door, then changed into the suit. There was a mirror on the back of the door, so she scrutinized herself for the first time in months.

The suit had a modest neckline but was cut really low in the back and high on the thighs. It clung to her every curve, making her realize just how much weight she'd lost. Her breasts had always been full and her waist small, but her hips had been too rounded for her liking. Now everything was trim to the point of thinness, and she wasn't sure she liked that, either.

"Oh, well," she said, frowning at the untidy strands of hair curling around her face. It was a fine, pale blonde that had grown well beyond shoulder length, and there were always a few tendrils that refused confinement. Susan tried to smooth them as she studied her face more critically.

Her color was a far cry from healthy even though she had a light tan. Her high-boned cheeks were thin to the point of gauntness but there wasn't anything she could do about that, either.

Maybe Doc Peters was right. Maybe a few days of rest would put some color in her face and fade the shadows beneath her eyes. She wanted to be strong and healthy again in mind, heart and body. If she was going to marry Luke and start a family, she had to take better care of herself.

If? Was there still doubt in her mind? Luke had already put the wheels in motion, but did she really want to make that sort of commitment? Permanent? Forever? 'Til death? She'd repeated vows with Shane, but the ceremony had been a travesty. The words had never come from her heart.

Could she succeed with Luke? Could she gamble her future in hopes of winning the home and family she so desperately craved? Or would this be another dismal failure? Worse yet, if she grew to love Luke, would she lose him, too?

Cornflower blue eyes, dulled somewhat from her exhaustion, were reflected in the mirror, their depths troubled with indecision.

"Oh, Mother, how I wish you were here," she whispered. Sometimes she missed her mother so much she didn't think she could bear it. Tears welled instantly in her eyes, but she drew once again on her hard-won control to force them back. There had been so many times over the past few years when she'd needed her mother's guidance and support. So many times when she mourned, all over again, the loss of her parents, their strength and stability.

She was so alone. For a woman who'd been a vivacious, fun-loving teenager and young adult, it was horribly painful to be so alone. She hated needing someone so much, yet she couldn't deny the truth. She needed Luke. She needed his home, his strength, his affection.

It might be a long time before they could ever totally trust each other and even longer before they could learn to love each other, but Susan made herself a vow to try as hard as humanly possible. If he tried even half as much, they could do it.

She had to try. She couldn't bear being alone any longer. Even if Luke wasn't wildly in love with her, she trusted him. He was a strong, honest, dependable man. They could learn to care for each other and create their own supportive family.

"Hey, did you fall in?" asked Rosa, interrupting her reverie. "Or do you need a different size?"

Susan smiled. She liked Rosa, her musical Spanish accent and her sense of humor. Being a part of Luke's household was already making her feel better.

"This one will be fine," she said, returning to the pantry and the waiting housekeeper. "I think it's a size smaller than I usually wear, but I don't have much meat on me right now anyway."

"Pretty skinny," the older woman announced, giving her the once-over. "You look like a half-starved fashion model, but at least you have some bosom and that suit makes your legs look longer. My home cooking will take care of the rest of the curves in no time at all."

"I have weird tan lines," Susan complained about the faint marks on her arms and neck.

"A little sun will change that, but go easy and use some sunscreen." Rosa dug through a cupboard and came up with a bottle of lotion and a beach towel. "Now give me your clothes and go relax. I'll bring you something cold to drink in a little while."

Once again Susan found herself obeying without argument. She was feeling drained again and welcomed a chance to lay her head down for a little bit.

The pool was Olympic size and took up a good section of the backyard. A security fence enclosed the entire patio and concrete deck around the pool. Several cushioned lounge chairs were on the deck, so she pulled one close to the water and sat down on it.

She'd take a dip when she felt a little more rested. After applying some sunscreen, she stretched out on the chaise. It was really comfortable and the sun felt wonderful. She pulled the stretchy band from her hair so that she could lay her head down flat, and within minutes she was sound asleep.

Some time later that sleep brought her incredibly erotic dreams. She had the total, undivided attention of a faceless, nameless man who came for no other reason than to please her. It began with a massage by strong hands using warm, fragrant oil.

He started with her toes and then inched his way over the ball of her foot to her arch. His thumbs worked magic as they gently but firmly stroked her instep until she felt a warm tingling sensation creep up her spine.

First one foot and then the other received highly focused attention. Susan heard herself moan with pleasure as more ripples of sensual bliss bombarded her. The hands moved slowly up her calves, rubbing and caressing muscle and flesh until every nerve ending in her body was alive with seductive heat.

Her thighs were especially sensitive and the hands stroked them with a liquid heat that set her on fire. She whimpered and shifted her legs in little, restless twitches. Then the hands had her hands, caressing each ringless finger, her thumbs and palms. Her arms were molded and stroked until her toes curled and a whole new sort of tension invaded her body.

She whimpered again softly when the palms of his hands skimmed over her ribs and lightly across her breasts, bringing her nipples into aching fullness with just the briefest touch.

When the callused yet tender hands kneaded her shoulders, caressed her neck and finally cupped her face, an image of a face behind the hands began to form. Susan lifted her heavy lids and looked directly into deep-set gray eyes that were watching her with such shattering intensity it stole what was left of her breath.

Luke's upper body was shading her eyes from the sun, so she had no problem seeing his face beneath the rim of his Stetson. His features were totally devoid of emotion, making it impossible to gauge his reaction to touching her so freely.

"You're going to get burned," was all he said as he took more of the lotion into his hands.

There were a lot of ways to get burned, but Susan couldn't worry about them now. She just felt—alive, aware, aroused. She tried to drag herself to alertness, but she was dazed by the blatant sensuality of his ministrations.

His hands continued to massage her cheeks, his thumbs at her temples. Then his fingers slid into her hair, combing it from her face before he moved his fingertips to massage her scalp.

She carefully studied his face as he concentrated on his self-appointed task. If he was as shaken by the contact as she was, he didn't show it.

"Turn over and I'll do your back," he commanded, his tone low but completely controlled.

Her expression told him she didn't know if she could bear any more of his erotic attentions, but he ignored the message and gently helped her turn onto her stomach.

She was wide awake now, yet the sensation of floating in a dreamlike state remained with her as his hands worked a similar magic on her shoulders, back and hips.

By the time he'd spread the sunscreen over the backs of her thighs, every nerve ending in her body was quivering with unrestrained excitement.

He grasped her hips and helped her turn so that she was facing him again. Susan felt as boneless and limp as a dishrag. She could only stare at him in mute fascination at his effortless manipulation of her senses.

Luke had been hunched down beside her, but stood to his full height and seemed especially tall from her vantage point. He was still dressed in his work clothes but his eyes were hidden from her as he looked down on her.

"Rosa suggested I bring you lemonade and remind you to put on more sunscreen," he explained.

Apparently he'd decided to take the housekeeper's suggestions to a higher level. She knew she must look like a wanton at the very least. He'd managed to thoroughly arouse her.

A glance at his jeans proved he was aroused, too, but in firm control of his desires. He obviously didn't intend to take his seduction any further, even though she just as obviously wouldn't object.

Her voice, when she tried to speak, was no more than a thready whisper. Pushing up on her elbows, she reached for the lemonade he'd placed on a nearby table. A sip of it helped clear her throat and she voiced the only coherent thought that came to mind.

"Thank you."

She was thanking him for his unselfish attentions, and for remaining in control when some men would have taken advantage of her vulnerability.

"My pleasure," he told her, though his tone didn't echo the sentiment, "but it might be best if we wait until we're married. You need to regain some strength."

Was this some form of sensual harassment, Susan wondered? Did he hope to make her want him so badly that she'd forget everything else? If so, she had to admit that his efforts were successful. She was aching.

Luke was aching too, but he was determined to fight the physical need. Kissing and caressing Susan this morning had temporarily thrown him off balance. Her passionate response had created a deep sensual hunger that threatened his control. Caressing her just now had been an exercise in restraint, but a painfully arousing one.

It had also proven what he'd always suspected. She was a deeply sensual woman who loved the feel of a man's hands on her body. Her soft moans had been genuine. The sight of her fat, hard nipples pressing against the fabric of her suit was more evidence of her lush sensuality. His muscles clenched at the thought, and he was suddenly impatient to have things settled between them.

"Granddad's seventy-fifth birthday party is a week from today. I'd like to be married by then. That way we can announce it to the family and friends all at once. Get it over with and get on with our lives."

Susan was trying to get her wayward emotions under control. It was difficult to concentrate on what he was saying even though she knew it was incredibly important.

"Couldn't we just announce our engagement next Saturday?"

His eyes flared. "You still have doubts?"

"No." Her reply was truthful. Everything was just happening so fast.

"Then there's no point waiting. I'd like to have Granddad stand up with me, if he's willing, but the rest of the family can find out about it after it's done."

She'd lost contact with most her old school friends and didn't feel close to anyone. "Will I need a maid of honor?"

"Just someone to act as a witness."

"What exactly are you planning?"

"Rosa wants a celebration, but I told her it'd have to be a private one. She had a fit when I suggested bringing Judge Anderson out here, but says Reverend Thompson would probably be happy to do the service.

"If we have him perform the service, we'll have to attend counseling first," Luke continued. "It's up to you."

She and Shane had been married in the judge's chambers with only his staff as witnesses. This time she wanted to be married by a minister.

"I'd like to ask Reverend Thompson."

Luke nodded his approval. "We can see him after we get blood tests on Monday. As soon as we apply for a license the information goes on public record, not to mention the gossip mill. We'd better do that and have the ceremony Friday evening. We'll hear fewer complaints from everyone if it's official before they hear about it."

Susan agreed. She was suddenly anxious to make their relationship official, but she wasn't looking forward to all the bitterness the union would cause.

Shane's sister Linda would undoubtedly be the worst. The other woman had doted on her brother and helped to spoil him rotten. She'd been jealous of Susan, then devastated by Shane's illness and death.

Now she would be furious by a remarriage, especially to Luke. Like Shane, she'd believed her brother deserved more power and control within the family, even though he'd never done anything to earn it.

"Linda won't be shy about verbalizing her objections," she said aloud. "Even if she understands that it's mainly to keep Hanchart land intact."

He didn't deny it. "She'll raise hell, but not publicly," he told her. "She's too concerned about the family's image. She'll tell everyone you were so devastated by Shane's death that you married me on the rebound."

His tone had gone from indifferent to bitter. He was a proud man, and she supposed his ego would take a beating, but most people would understand his desire to protect his birthright.

"You're probably right. She'll need to explain why I re-married without at least a year of mourning. She'll tell her friends I couldn't bear to leave his home, that I'm trying to hang on to his memory, the Hanchart name, and social status."

That suggestion brought a tightening to Luke's already taut expression. Did he think the Hanchart name was all-important to her? Did he think she was marrying him on the rebound? Because she missed Shane so desperately? How important was it to let the truth be known? She didn't want to explain her relationship with Shane to him or anyone else. Explaining would mean revealing the secret she was desperate to keep.

"I do love this ranch," she wanted to clarify her position, feeling she owed him that, "but my decision to go through with the marriage has nothing to do with Shane or the family's social status. Can you believe that?"

He continued to stare into her eyes. It was clear that he doubted her motives, as well.

"I guess time will tell, won't it?"

"Time will tell what?" chimed another, older voice.

John Hanchart was joining them on the deck from the patio area. He'd overheard the end of the conversation and interrupted them with a question of his own. "What will time tell us?"

Luke's grandfather was tall and straight in posture with a head of thick, snow-white hair. His face was a road map of age lines, but his eyes were still as keen as his grandson's. They missed very little.

"Hi, Susan. It's a surprise to see you relaxing for a change." His smile of welcome was genuine. "A pleasant surprise." He was another member of the ranch family who frequently told her she worked too hard.

She sat up and swung her legs to the deck, but when she started to rise from the chaise, he waved her back down. "Don't get up on my account. Rosa says you had a bad spell and need to rest."

"Rosa's a mother hen."

"Rosa's right," added Luke. "Susan's under doctor's orders to slow down and get some rest."

"Makes sense to me," John decided, tossing his towel on a nearby chair. "So what will time be telling us?"

Luke glanced at her, and then turned more fully toward John. "Susan and I have decided to get married as soon as we can arrange a ceremony. It won't be a popular decision with the rest of the family, but they'll have to get used to the idea whether they like it or not."

John's eyes narrowed as he considered the two of them and offered a short, terse lecture. "I can see where marriage would offer a practical solution to your problems, but I hope you're not going into it with the intention of divorcing when it's convenient.

"There's never been a divorce in the Hanchart family. There've been lots of different reasons for marriages over the generations, but once a commitment was made, it was upheld," he declared. "Marriage is a serious, lifetime commitment. Are you just sealing a business agreement or are you planning to have a real marriage?"

"Real." They chorused in unison.

John studied them both a little longer, and then seemed satisfied with what he saw. "In that case, you've got my blessing," he said. His tone lightened and his eyes took on a devilish gleam. "I'll even dance at the wedding."

Susan could almost feel Luke relax. She knew that although he was a powerful man in his own right, he respected his grandfather and wanted his support.

"I'll need a best man," he added quietly, his eyes warming as they met John's. "Think you could do the honors?"

For just an instant, Susan was certain the older man would be overcome with emotion. He swiftly blinked his eyes, and then grinned widely and threw an arm around Luke's shoulders.

"Damn, boy, you know I've been trying to marry you off for years. You bet I'll be best man. I'll come with bells on."

Susan smiled as the men gave each other a rare hug. Then John's eyes were pivoting to her. "I hope this boy of mine told you I want about ten great-grandbabies."

She felt herself blushing, but managed to return his teasing. "Actually, he mentioned a dozen, but these things take time."

John roared with laughter, and she was thrilled to see a smile on Luke's face. With his grandfather he seemed younger, more carefree and relaxed. There was no problem communicating or a noticeable generation gap.

Is that the type of family man he was? Tough as nails when it was necessary, but soft as a marshmallow when it came to those he loved? The thought brought a yearning in her so intense that it hurt. Her chest tightened. What would it be like to be loved by such a man? To be the center of Luke's attention?

Did she dare even wonder? If she allowed herself to dream, it might only bring more heartache. Dreams had a way of going astray.

"What about you, Susan? Who'll stand up with you?" John asked.

She glanced at Luke. "Do you think Rosa would mind?"

The men shared a grin. "Do babies cry?" John teased. "That woman loves any reason to celebrate. She's spent the last month planning a surprise party for me. I don't want one, but I hate to disappoint her."

Susan grinned. "If it's a surprise party, you're not supposed to know about it."

"It's hard not to know when she's had one every year for the last twenty. I keep complaining and she keeps on doing just what she wants. Says she needs to be busy, and I need coddling. Says it's a family tradition. Maybe now that you're coming to stay, she'll leave me in peace."

Susan's laughter was light and musical, charming both men with the sweet rarity of it. "I'm sure she's capable of coddling both of us."

"I suppose," he grumbled. "She'll be out here any minute now wondering if we have something cold to drink, if we remembered to use sunscreen or if we need a snack to sustain us until dinner."

John had his own small house a mile down the road, but he often took his evening meal with Luke. He swore that Rosa would smother him if he didn't keep his distance for the rest of the day.

"I'm going back to work," Luke told them. "The two of you can deal with Rosa yourselves."

"Why don't you change and swim with us a while," John asked him. "The work'll still be there later."

"I just came in to get a jug of tea for the men," Luke explained. "Rosa'll have it ready by now."

"Suit yourself," said his grandfather. "But you won't find better company than ours, will he, Susan?"

She tactfully avoided answering the question. "I'm finding the water pretty hard to resist, myself. I think I'll get in and cool off a little."

"Just remember to stay in the shade when you're done," Luke warned, his eyes following her long-legged saunter to the edge of the pool. "You're already starting to get burned."

"I'll remember," she tossed over her shoulder before making a clean, graceful dive into the water.

The two men watched as her head surfaced and she began to swim with long, sure strokes.

"She's one hell of a woman," John told his grandson. "I've watched her work around here, and she's a natural with the horses. She's smart and dependable and trustworthy."

"Strong recommendation coming from an old widower like you."

"Damned straight. If I were fifty years younger, I'd give you a run for your money and take special care with her. She's had a rough time. I don't know why she married Shane, but I'd be willing to bet your inheritance that it was a bad marriage from start to finish."

Luke stared at his grandfather for a long while, his expression thoughtful. There was very little that meant more to John Hanchart than the family's ranch, and he didn't make light of bets on it. He was dead serious about Susan's marriage. Only time would tell if he was right about it.

Chapter Four

ൟ

Susan was amazed at how much she could actually sleep once she'd followed the doctor's orders to relax. She slept soundly Saturday night, even in a strange bed. Always an early riser, she was up early the next day, but then she dozed off again beside the pool.

Part of the reason she was able to rest was due to having a definite course of action for her future. Now that she knew what direction her life was going to take, it was easier to make the psychological adjustments. Luke had lifted a heavy burden from her shoulders with his proposal.

He'd given her a whole new set of worries, of course, but they were different. They offered a challenge that she was happy to accept. She knew she had her work cut out for her to make a success of their relationship, but she didn't mind challenges.

Other than their confrontation in the barn and his erotic massage, he'd made himself scarce. She didn't know if he kept his distance so that she could relax or if he thought their volatile reaction to each other could cause problems.

Maybe he was old-fashioned enough to disapprove of premarital sex. She would agree on that, but knew he'd never believe her. He assumed that she and Shane had shared a normal, loving relationship.

He would have to learn the truth, but she wasn't sure how to broach the subject. Maybe, just maybe, they could enter into a relationship without him realizing how inexperienced she really was.

He certainly knew how to arouse her. Maybe, if she was really lucky, he would excite her to the point that she didn't freeze when he tried to consummate their marriage. Maybe he could block the horror of Shane's attack from her mind long enough to let nature take its course. Maybe. There were a lot of ifs and maybes, but she was trying to think positively.

John joined her again by the pool on Sunday afternoon. Along with his beach towel, he carried a large dress box. Susan greeted him with a smile and some teasing.

"Have you been shopping this morning?"

He grinned, tossed his towel on the deck and laid the box on the end of a lounge chair.

"Nope. This was over at my place. I brought it here to show you."

Interest piqued, she rose from her chair and watched as he cut through the sealing tape with his pocketknife. The box showed signs of age and had apparently been in storage for a long time.

"What is it?"

"Come see," he invited, opening the box and carefully spreading the tissue paper.

She joined him and then gasped with delight as he unveiled a beautifully preserved wedding gown. He lifted it from its bed of tissue and gently shook out the folds.

"Oh, John, it's gorgeous!"

Her hands were damp, so she didn't want to touch the delicate ivory satin, but he held it, turning it so she could see it from every angle. The length was mid-calf with a scalloped hemline. It had elbow-length fitted sleeves and a vee-neck trimmed in delicate Victorian lace. The bodice was covered in tiny seed pearls, and she loved it on sight.

"Alma's mother made this gown by hand," he explained, speaking of his deceased wife. "She wore it for our wedding fifty-five years ago. I promised her I'd keep it cleaned and preserved until Luke took a bride. She doted on that boy, you know," he reminisced. "Since the two of you are to be married, I thought I'd see if you'd like to borrow it for the ceremony."

Susan's eyes widened in surprise. She knew that John had adored his Alma. Memories of her still seemed to touch him deeply and his gesture touched her. She hadn't even considered the need for a wedding dress. Her wardrobe was woefully lacking of anything special.

When she didn't say anything for a minute, he continued, "She was a hopeless romantic, and she wouldn't have wanted you to wear it unless you really like it, but I thought I'd make the offer for her."

"It's the most beautiful gown I've ever seen, and I love it," she insisted. "But we're going to have a very small, quiet ceremony."

"You and Luke said it'll be a real marriage, so you might as well have a real wedding. It doesn't have to be big, but it can be special."

Susan was almost too overcome with emotion to speak. She didn't know what Luke would think about her wearing his grandmother's gown, but no woman in her right mind could resist such temptation.

"It's perfect," she whispered. "I would be more than honored to wear it, if you're absolutely sure you wouldn't mind."

"No, no," he said, clearing his voice and trying not to let emotion get the best of him. "I wouldn't have offered it if I had any objections. I told Rosa I'd be bringin' it. She said she'll make any alterations you need."

"John, you're absolutely sure? I don't want to damage the dress with alterations. What if I stain it or something?"

"It's not much use if nobody's ever going to wear it again," he added practically as he replaced the dress in the folds of tissue paper and then closed the lid. "It's time I let somebody else worry about preservin' the damn thing."

"Oh, John, thank you!" was all she could manage. She threw her arms around him and hugged him fiercely.

The old man chuckled and awkwardly patted her back in response. Susan didn't want to make him feel uncomfortable, so she made a concerted effort to control herself.

"My parents used to tease me about getting married," she said as she eased from his arms. "Daddy used to say he'd supply the stepladder and help me elope, but Mother made all these elaborate plans for a big, formal wedding. She would have loved Alma's gown."

Her voice cracked on the last words, and she knew she needed a little privacy to regain control. "I think I'll take it up to my room, if you don't mind."

"Go right ahead, but don't forget to come back and swim with me. I'm old, and I need supervision."

His teasing brought an answering smile to her face, a smile that competed with the sun for its brilliance. Her eyes sparkled like the rarest of sapphires, and her exquisite beauty was enough to steal a man's breath.

It was that smile she turned on Luke as he came striding onto the pool deck to join them. It stopped him in his tracks. For a long moment all he did was stare at her while a high-voltage electrical energy crackled between them.

Susan was sure she'd be singed by the fire that leapt to his eyes. When she was finally able to drag in a steadying breath, she scooped up the dress box and held it defensively in front of her, as though it offered protection from the heat of his gaze.

"I'll take this upstairs and be right back," she managed, leaving them on trembling legs.

It was hard to believe how deeply affected she was by nothing more than a searing glance from the man she'd promised to marry. How could she hope to cope with his full attention when just his undiluted interest left her trembling?

She took the beautiful dress to her room and hung it on a padded hanger, stroking the satin with loving fingers. John's generosity made her feel weepy, but she fought off the melancholy and returned to the pool.

He and Luke were in the water. They'd stretched a volleyball net across one end of the pool and were batting a ball back and forth. John was in excellent condition for a man his age, but Luke was truly awesome, with shoulders that seemed impossibly wide and tightly corded muscles that rippled with his every movement.

John grabbed the ball when it came zinging his way and paused to yell at Susan. "Hey, I need some help here. I'm too old to keep up with this big kid much longer."

She grinned when he referred to Luke as a kid since he was one hundred percent adult male in thinking and physique. "I'll help, but I'm not sure how much," she warned.

The men didn't mind. They seemed to enjoy her company, and she enjoyed theirs as they laughed and teased and played. It was a rare pleasure for her to be part of a family again, even a small one. She couldn't remember the last time she'd actually played a game or laughed so much. She basked in the simple joy of it.

Later she put together a light meal for the three of them since Rosa didn't work on Sunday. When Luke excused himself from their company to attend to paperwork, John spent a couple hours trying to teach her how to play chess. She'd always admired the older man, but the more time she spent with him the more she grew to like him.

It was nearly ten o'clock when they put away the chess set. John said it was past his bedtime, and that he'd stick his head in the office to tell Luke they were calling it a night. She worried a little about her future husband's reluctance to spend time with her, but refused to dwell on it too much. For the second night in a row she was sound asleep within minutes of climbing into bed.

On Monday morning Luke took her to Doctor Peters' office for a checkup while he ran some errands. Then they had blood drawn and headed back to the ranch. Reverend Thompson paid them a visit in the afternoon, counseled them on the ups and downs of married life and then scheduled the wedding service for early Friday evening.

When he left, they remained in the ranch office for a few minutes. The room was big and sparsely furnished with a desk, some file cabinets and three brown leather chairs. The carpet and furniture were serviceable so that any dirt tracked in could be easily removed.

Luke moved behind his desk, sat down and handed a postcard-sized form to Susan. "This is a signature card from the bank," he explained. "I talked to Bob Anderson today and told him we were getting married. He can be trusted to keep quiet about it, but he needs your signature for your bank account."

Susan studied the form. She'd closed her account as well as Shane's. "What account?"

"I'm opening a new checking account for you, and he needs your signature so you can access the ranch's operating account. Rosa, Juan and I all have access to the business one. For your personal account, you'll have checking, ATM and credit card access once it's all processed."

She couldn't help but stare at him in amazement. "I don't want access to your money," she argued.

Luke's mouth stretched into a tight line. "As of Friday it'll be our money, remember? You'll need an allowance, and I'll have to transfer a large sum of money into your personal account to pay Shane's bills."

Susan responded through tight lips. Determined to be totally truthful with him, she explained that Shane's debts had been accrued from gambling as well as medical expenses and that he shouldn't have to pay for his cousin's bad habits.

"You shouldn't be saddled with them either, but you are and I'll consider them my responsibility once we're married."

"I know those debts need to be paid," she said. Pride kept her from graciously accepting anything more from him. "But I don't need an allowance or access to the ranch account. I'm not bringing a penny into the marriage."

He frowned. "Your dowry is the Hanchart land."

"But I can't legally turn that over to you." At least not until she found some other way around the terms of Shane's will.

"I'm not asking you to," he replied in a clipped tone. "I'll fight you to the death if you ever try to walk away and take any of it with you. But once we're married you become part owner of everything."

She took his words in the manner he intended them—as a threat. He wasn't demanding a prenuptial agreement on paper, but he was demanding it just the same.

"I don't have any aspirations to make off with what has belonged to your family for generations." In fact, she was determined to find some other way around the terms of Shane's will. Some way to permanently give the land back to the Hanchart family even if things between her and Luke didn't work out in the long term.

"Good because I have no intention of giving up even a fraction of it."

They stared at each other for a long time, both tense with frustration. Shane was, and probably always would be, at the root of their problems, yet they had to find a way to deal with the mess he'd created.

"You're also bringing the promise of future generations of Hancharts to this marriage," he reminded. "That's important."

He left little doubt that the land was his primary concern, and any future they built was secondary. The idea sent a little shiver of dread down her spine.

"And what if I can't follow through on the promise?" she wanted to know. "If we find out I'm not any good at procreating, will I just get tossed out on my ear?"

She could tell by the tightening of his jaw that he wasn't pleased by the question or her refusal to cooperate.

"We're talking about a real marriage, remember? That point seems to be getting by you," was his grating comeback. "If one of us isn't capable of engendering a child then we consider the options. Just like any other couple would do."

Susan sighed heavily and ran her fingers through her hair. It was hanging straight and loose around her shoulders today, so she had to keep shoving it back to keep it off her face.

"I'm sorry, Luke. I want a real marriage too. I'm just having a hard time adjusting to all the details."

His tone was hard when he answered. "It's not the first time for you. You should be more familiar with the routine than I am," he reminded, expression hard.

She couldn't refute the truth of them. She wished she could explain how different this was and how much more important it was to her. She wondered if he'd ever get over his resentment of her first marriage.

"I never handled any of our finances when Shane and I were married," was her weak reply.

Shane had wanted her totally dependent on him. He'd provided a cash allowance for groceries and had taken care of everything else when it suited him. The only spending money she'd ever had was what she'd earned teaching some riding classes.

"You won't have to handle anything now if you don't want to," he told her, "but you're bound to need money at some point."

Susan nodded in agreement, but she didn't feel very agreeable. She felt like a freeloader. A complete fraud. The parasite people would call her when they learned she'd married him.

She didn't want a penny of his money, not even to lift the crushing load of debt Shane had dropped on her shoulders. She wasn't sure what it felt like to be a real wife, but all she felt right now was cheap.

The only thing she could do was sign the forms to avoid another argument. She couldn't prevent his grim anger about her previous marriage, but she would try be more cooperative. She picked up a pen and filled out the signature card.

Luke took the form, read her name and then gave her a strange look. His expression was questioning, making her brows furrow in a frown.

"What's wrong? Did I sign the wrong line?"

His gaze never left her face. "You signed your maiden name, Lawrie."

Susan felt warmth creep into her cheeks. She wasn't being deliberately obtuse, she just wasn't thinking clearly. She'd never really thought of herself as a Hanchart, so she'd never gotten into the habit of using the name.

"I'm sorry, Luke, I didn't think about it," she said. "I swear I didn't do it on purpose. Will they accept that or can we get another form?"

"It can wait," he replied, crushing the paper and tossing it in the trash can. "Once we're married you can get used to signing as Mrs. Luke Hanchart."

The accent on his first name held more than a hint of possessiveness. It troubled her. She didn't want him feeling like he had to compete with his dead cousin. Not on her account. Not for any reason.

"In the meantime, let me know if you need money for anything," he added.

Her reply was swift. "I don't need any money."

Luke's eyes bored into hers. He wondered what kind of game she was playing. She was obviously broke, so why pretend she didn't need his money?

"Clothes? Personal items?" She was shaking her head. "Rosa said you didn't unpack many clothes. Do you have the rest stored?"

Susan felt her blush deepen, in her younger days she'd been a real clotheshorse. She'd owned more clothes and shoes than she'd had room for in her closets, but most of them were gone now. She'd sold her best outfits to help support Butch in the lean years. They hadn't brought a lot of money, but every penny had been needed.

Shane had liked to show her off to his friends, so he'd bought several flashy outfits for her. She'd hated them and had given them all to charity after he died. The whole issue was a sore subject.

"Unless you're planning on doing a lot of entertaining, I don't need dressy clothes. I have plenty of jeans and shirts."

"How about the party Saturday night?"

"I have a couple of decent outfits," she snapped. "I'll try not to embarrass you."

"Dammit, that's not what I meant and you know it. You're just being bullheaded again."

"And you're being insulting."

"I'm trying to take care of your needs. That's what husbands do, or so I'm told."

Susan was torn. She didn't want to argue anymore. She ran a hand over her eyes and drew in a deep breath. They were both getting testy, and that was counterproductive.

"I don't need anything right now," she told him very honestly and firmly.

"I hope you're not planning to go back to work at the restaurant." The subject added more annoyance to his tone. "I need you here with the horses."

"I told you I was replaced, and I prefer working with the horses," she replied, even though he seemed to be managing just fine without her help. "Once we're married I'll sign the proper name on the proper forms and help myself to your money. Okay?"

It was obvious that he didn't appreciate her tone or attitude. Her weak attempt at humor failed miserably. She could almost see the wheels of his brain turning as he searched for hidden meanings in everything she said.

His suspicious attitude hurt even though she understood the cause. It was sad to think he had to question the motives of everyone he dealt with, even on a personal level. If that was what it meant to have lots of money and power, she wasn't interested in either.

However he interpreted her words, he decided not to argue any further. His eyes never left hers as he replied. "I guess it'll have to do for now, won't it?"

"I guess it will."

* * * * *

It was Wednesday morning before Susan ventured out of the house again. Luke had assured her the horses were being taken care of, but she wanted to spend some time with them herself. She waited until he and most of the ranch hands went to round up cattle, then she headed for the broodmare barn.

Unfortunately, the man in charge of feeding the mares was Rod Matthews. He was her least favorite of Shane's old friends, the one she'd chased from the house with a shotgun. The sight of him halted her in her tracks.

Rod's uncle was the Matthews who'd tried to buy Shane's land from her. He was very wealthy and Rod was his only living relative, yet the two of them were always feuding. He usually came to work for the Hancharts when his uncle got fed up with him. Rod was very much like Shane had been—handsome, spoiled and totally lacking in morals.

He turned as soon as he caught sight of her and flashed her a hundred-watt smile that might have thrilled some women, but not her.

"Mornin', Susan." Setting aside the feed pail, he began to move slowly toward her with a smug expression and a much-practiced swagger.

Tall, dark and handsome, he was very good-looking but had an ego bigger than Texas. They'd known each other since grade school. He'd been a bully and she a defender of those he bullied.

"Haven't seen you out and about much lately."

"I came to check on the horses," was her cool reply. She tried to move past him, but he stuck out an arm to block her path. She was loath to touch him, even long enough to shove his arm out of her way.

"What's the hurry, widow lady?" His snicker was barely camouflaged by the low drawl. "You got no shotgun and nobody around to interfere, so why not pass the time with some pleasantries?"

Susan didn't want any part of his sort of pleasantries. "Get out of my way, Rod."

His eyes flashed. "Now, now, watch your tone, spitfire. That ain't no way to get a man like me to cooperate," he told her. "You need honey, not vinegar."

She just glared at him, and he continued.

"I thought you was all packed up and movin' to the big city," he said. "Or was that just a ruse to get an invite from Luke to share the big house?"

She didn't dignify the question with a response, but her expression told him that it was none of his business.

"You sharin' his bed too?"

"You're disgusting," she snapped. "Get out of my way."

"Make me, sugar," he persisted, eyes gleaming with unholy pleasure. "I'd sure welcome a chance to rassle around with you a while."

Susan wasn't about to accept the challenge. She knew his ego was still smarting from earlier rejections, so she decided to retreat and come back later. But when she turned to leave the barn, he grabbed her by the shoulders and twisted her backward into his arms.

The action startled and unbalanced her. Before she could react with any force, he had her shoved against the wall with her arms pinned. Fighting to free herself from his oppressive strength, she twisted and kicked out at him, but her efforts were wasted.

When he started to lower his head, she screamed in frustrated fury, "Stop it! Damn you, stop it!"

He tried to kiss her, but she threw her head from side to side to avoid his mouth. When he let go of her arms long enough to hold her head still she slapped him on both sides of his head, hard enough to make his ears ring.

"Vicious bitch," he rasped, clutching her arms so hard they went numb. He shook his head as if to clear it. "Shane always said you liked to play rough."

"Shane was a liar, and you're nothing but slime!" she screamed. The suffocating press of his body against hers was stirring her into a panic, and she fought for breath.

Then Luke appeared behind Rod, and she was suddenly free. He spun the younger man around and landed a solid right fist on Rod's jaw. It was followed by another fist to the stomach. The blows sent him to his knees.

"Get up!" Luke snarled in rage.

Rod came off the floor with the speed of a snake, lunging for him, but he was no match for Luke's superior size and strength. After another fist connected with his face, he went down again.

Luke would have dragged him to his feet for more punches, but Rod quickly rolled out of reach.

"I got no quarrel with you," he insisted, holding his stomach and gasping for air.

Luke didn't respond to that. "Get up, get your gear packed and be off my property in an hour. I'll send your pay, but if I ever catch you on Hanchart property again I'll tear you apart."

Rod was obviously stunned to find himself fired. "You can't mean that," he argued, brushing a shirtsleeve over his bleeding lip. "I'm one of the best hands on this ranch and you know it."

Luke's reply was terse. "I've warned you before and I'm done warning. You're nothing but trouble. Now get out before I throw you out!"

Rod came to his feet, scooped his hat from the floor and slapped it on his head. "You'll be sorry for this," he warned. With that and a malevolent glance at Susan, he strode angrily from the barn.

She was still visibly shaken. Her knees had collapsed under her when Luke pulled Rod away, but she rose and steadied herself with a hand on the wall. Her breathing was a little ragged and she was fighting for control.

She hated being the cause of trouble between Luke and one of his ranch hands. It was humiliating and unfair. It wasn't her fault the cowboy was an arrogant jerk.

Luke's eyes were turbulent as he turned them on her. "Did he hurt you?" he asked, making no move to comfort her.

"No." She'd been furious, scared, and furious for being scared. But she was unharmed. "Not really."

Her response seemed to refuel his anger. "What the hell's been going on here?" he demanded.

Susan stiffened in resentment. She understood that he was upset by the situation, but any fool could see she wasn't happy about it, either. Did he think she'd encouraged the attack? Was he blaming her for the necessity of firing one of his best employees?

"I just came out to check on the horses." She refused to defend herself for Rod's disgusting attitude.

"You didn't invite his attention?"

Her eyes narrowed in anger. "What do you think?"

His jaw tightened when she answered his question with one of her own. His eyes still blazed with anger, but he turned his back and followed Rod from the barn without another word.

Susan was trembling uncontrollably now. She laid her arm on top of Mariado's stall and rested her head on her forearm. Forcing herself to take deep, calming breaths, she slowly regained some control.

She didn't think all of Luke's anger was directed at her, yet his attitude hurt. She would have appreciated some measure of good faith. Surely he wasn't small-minded enough to believe she'd deliberately provoked Rod?

He would have to believe what he wanted. She hadn't initiated the argument and she didn't see any way she could have prevented what happened. Her only recourse would be to stay locked indoors all the time.

She did feel guilty about Luke losing a valued employee. Experienced help was hard to find and keep in these parts, but she was still relieved to have Rod gone. She only hoped the other man wouldn't continue to cause trouble.

Chapter Five

ဢ

By the time Susan began preparing for the wedding ceremony on Friday evening, she was a bundle of nerves. Besides all the usual last-minute doubts, she had a severe case of jitters.

Luke had been more reserved than usual throughout the week. He hadn't mentioned the incident in the barn again, but he'd worked incredibly long hours and kept as much distance between them as possible.

They'd had very few conversations, and those had been limited to discussions about the horses. They'd shared meals and the house like casual acquaintances. Within half an hour, they'd be married. For better or worse.

"Susan, you look absolutely beautiful!" Rosa exclaimed once she was dressed and ready. Alma's gown hadn't required too much alteration.

"Thank you, but the gown is beautiful all by itself."

Rosa tut-tutted at her modesty and continued to smooth and pat folds and lace until she was certain everything was just perfect. Then she turned Susan around and made her look at her image in the mirror.

She'd acquired a deeper tan that set off the pearly color of the ivory against her skin. Rosa had pinned her hair up in a loose chignon. She'd drawn the line at wearing a veil for such an informal wedding, but Rosa hadn't been daunted. She'd made a wreath out of baby's breath and pinned it to her blonde tresses.

The heart-shaped locket at her throat had belonged to her great-grandmother, so it was very old. There was a delicate blue han-y tucked in her bra. The dress was borrowed, so Susan thought she had taken care of all the traditions.

It might seem silly to anyone else, but the little things were important to her. She would soon be making a once-in-a-lifetime commitment, and she needed all the moral fortification she could muster.

She looked like a bride. You are a bride, she silently chastised her own image, bringing an added blush to her pale cheeks. The circumstances of the marriage might be unusual, but she was feeling all the usual turmoil such a momentous commitment involved.

There was more than a little apprehension in the blue eyes regarding the bride's reflection in the mirror. What would Luke think of her? Would he be annoyed that she'd dressed so formally? That she was wearing a Hanchart heirloom?

Would he show up in normal work clothes and be embarrassed by her elegance? Would he repeat his vows and make himself scarce again? She hadn't found the nerve to discuss the details with him.

Rosa had baked a cake and been very secretive about the other preparations. Susan was told not to worry about anything. All she knew was the service would be held in the small flower garden on the west side of the house.

"It's almost time to go downstairs," said Rosa. "Are you ready?"

Susan mustered a smile even though her insides ware quivering like jelly. "I guess."

Rosa relayed a message to her husband, Juan, outside the bedroom door, and then the women followed him downstairs. Juan was only an inch or so taller than his wife. He was a thin man who blamed his growing potbelly on her cooking. He had a head full of thick, graying hair and dark eyes that danced with perpetual good humor.

Those eyes smiled with encouragement as they reached the double doors to the garden. Then Juan lifted a florist's box, and Rosa handed her a bouquet of yellow rosebuds.

"Oh, how thoughtful!" Susan exclaimed, giving them both a hug. "They're beautiful, and I love roses."

"Now you just stand here a minute until I take my place near the reverend," Rosa advised. "You can start through the doors when the music starts."

"Music?" Susan repeated in surprise, but Rosa and Juan were already zipping out the doors.

Then she heard the beginning strains of the Wedding March. For just an instant her heart leapt to her throat, the butterflies in her stomach fluttered wildly, and she was certain she couldn't move if her life depended on it.

She stifled a sob of surprise at the housekeeper's romantic gesture, wishing more than ever that her parents could be with her today. Then the doors were opening wide and more than a dozen cowboys rose to their feet and turned in her direction. The ranch hands were all wearing their Sunday best and looking expectantly toward her.

A small aisle had been cleared with rows of chairs on either side. A white cloth runner and wicker baskets bulging with fresh flowers marked the bride's path. Susan was bombarded with their heady scents. Her gaze flew the length of the aisle until it found Luke.

He stood at the minister's left, dressed in a dark blue suit with a white shirt. He was so striking her breath caught in her throat at the sight of him. Their gazes locked and his compelled her to finally move forward.

She started toward him, automatically keeping time to the slow, steady beat of the music. Her heart was thudding so hard it shook her body, and her pulse pounded in her ears with a deafening roar.

The short aisle was only a few yards long, but seemed to take an eternity to walk. Once she reached Luke's side, everyone turned their attention toward the minister. He motioned for the men to take their seats as the music faded to an end. Susan dragged in a long, steadying breath. Rosa reached for her bouquet, and she relinquished it.

The service itself was brief. Her voice was a little shaky at first, but grew more steady. Luke's was as strong and sure as always. When it came to the part where they were to exchange rings John handed a gold band to Luke. He slipped it on her cold, trembling finger.

Rosa provided the second gold band. Susan clasped it tightly, afraid she'd embarrass herself by dropping it. Luke held out his hand and she repeated the words "with this ring, I thee wed".

That was when she felt the faint tremor in his hands, and her gaze shot to his. For a long moment, everything and everyone faded, leaving only the two of them to stare into each other's eyes.

A brief instant of uncertainty in his gaze brought a sudden calm over Susan. Knowing that he was a little shaken, that he didn't take the ceremony lightly and that for once he wasn't totally in control of his emotions had a calming effect on hers.

"You're sure?" she mouthed the words so that only he could see.

In response, Luke lifted her hand to his mouth and placed a brief, warm kiss on the ring he'd just given her. In that instant, with his head bent over her hand and his mouth on her flesh, Susan realized how much she loved him. How much she needed him and wanted his love. Though she'd fought the knowledge for years, her heart began screaming the message so loudly she was sure the world could hear.

It was a shocking revelation and caused another tremor to pass over her. A whole host of emotions bombarded her as her lashes swept down to hide the sudden vulnerability she felt.

Along with the vulnerability came relief and a certainty that she'd made the right choice in marrying him. He might not love her, but he wanted a real marriage. She was more determined than ever to have one. The vows they were sharing were the most important in her life, and she told him as much with her eyes when she reopened them.

Luke's eyes darkened with emotion, but a discreet cough from Reverend Thompson redirected their attention. The rest of their vows were repeated in firm, steady tones.

When it was time for the groom to kiss his bride, he cupped her cheek in one big hand and gently lifted her face toward him. His kiss was swift and hard. It was a firm, almost impatient promise that made her knees weak.

Then Reverend Thompson introduced them as man and wife, and a loud cheer went up. Chaos reined for the next few minutes while congratulations were offered. Someone showered them with confetti.

Everyone shook the groom's hand and pounded him on the back, then kissed the bride. Susan shared hugs and kisses with Rosa, John and the rest of the ranch family.

She knew she'd never be able to tell them how much their special efforts meant to her. The gown, the music, the flowers were all a dream come true. It made her feel as though she really belonged here, as though she'd come home again. She silently promised to cherish what she'd found.

Luke was smiling and accepting congratulations along with some teasing from his men. She risked a glance at him, but couldn't maintain eye contact. Her newly discovered love left her feeling unsure and shy. A deeper blush colored her cheeks.

A flash of light heralded a round of picture-taking. One of the younger cowhands, named Toby, was a camera buff. He'd been commissioned to take wedding pictures.

"We'll be cutting the cake in the dining room," said Rosa. "There's food and drinks too." Her invitation started a small stampede into the house.

Toby took a few more pictures of the small wedding party and then everyone headed for the dining room.

The next couple hours passed with cutting the cake, sharing food with their guests and an abundance of champagne. Friday was payday, so Susan felt honored that the men had given up their usual night on the town to help them celebrate.

Rosa made sure their glasses were never empty and that beer was offered for those who preferred it. Juan grumbled that he'd never get any work out of them the next morning, but nobody seemed very concerned.

Susan was too nervous to eat much, but she drank her share of champagne. By nine o'clock she was beginning to feel the effects. Rosa, with Juan's help, prodded the partygoers to head for home. John said his good night, and the housekeeper insisted that the bride forget about the mess.

"But you've already done so much," Susan complained, "and you have a party tomorrow night."

"It's nothing," Rosa brushed aside her concerns while shooing her from the room. "I love it. It's still early and Juan will help. You go on up to bed. It's bad enough you won't get a long honeymoon. Take what time you can get."

The suggestion brought an immediate flush to Susan's face. Worries about her wedding night hadn't been far from her mind all evening, and she couldn't help being nervous. No amount of wine could completely drown her concerns.

Luke walked his grandfather home, so she decided to take advantage of his absence. She gave Rosa another hug, thanked her profusely and then headed for her bedroom.

What she found there gave her pause. The closet and drawers were empty. All her personal items were gone. A note from Rosa explained that everything had been moved to the master bedroom. Heat raced through her at the thought.

In the middle of the bed was a gift-wrapped box with a tag that bore Rosa's name. Inside was an exquisite yellow silk nightgown. Susan pulled it from the box, her heart racing again. Her wedding night and all its implications were finally hitting home.

Except for this evening, Luke hadn't kissed her or touched her in almost a week. What if he expected too much from her tonight? What if he expected her to be wise in the ways of men? Would he assume she'd know how to please him? He was expecting her to be sexually experienced, yet she wasn't. Would he be able to tell? Could it be faked?

There hadn't been an opportunity to discuss her limited experience with him. He probably wouldn't believe her anyway. She knew Shane used to boast about their adventures in bed even though there hadn't been any.

She slipped out of her wedding gown and hung it on a padded hanger until she could have it properly cleaned and stored. Then she took a quick shower and slipped into the nightgown Rosa had provided.

The silk slid over her body like a whisper, teasing her senses. The feel of it against her naked skin renewed the inner warmth that had been fluctuating from hot to hotter all evening.

Did all new brides feel this apprehensive? Or did knowing that her husband didn't love her make the difference? Her newly recognized love for him was certainly adding to her tension. Would he notice a change in her?

Should she know what to do now? Go to Luke's room and wait for him? Stay here and see if he'd come to her? How was she to know?

The decision was taken out of her hands with the sound of Luke leaving his room and crossing to hers. After a perfunctory knock he pushed open the door.

She felt like a virgin sacrifice, standing before him in nothing more than a wisp of silk that clung to moist spots all over her body. She hadn't brushed out her hair, so damp tendrils spilled from a crooked chignon onto her neck.

Luke had long since shed his suit jacket and rolled up the sleeves of his shirt. Now it was unbuttoned to the waist, giving her a glimpse of bronze muscle covered in golden hair. His eyes were bright and riveted on her.

She felt her nipples pucker with his continued perusal. Her stomach was already clenched in knots and all the rest of her began to tremble. She was certain her brain had lost command of her body.

He took a few steps into the room until they were within touching distance. Then he brought both hands up and cupped her breasts, brushing his thumbs over the pebbled tips until they ached with tightness.

Already flushed with fever, his touch induced an avalanche of heated energy. Susan had to lower her lashes to keep him from seeing how passionately her body responded to his feather-light touch.

The continued brush of silk and thumbs over her nipples caused her breasts to swell in painful need. She remembered the feel of his mouth on the same flesh and memory sent more heat spiraling toward her womb.

He didn't say anything for several long moments, just continued to caress her until her whole body was quivering and her knees started to wobble. She could feel his silvery eyes studying her face, but kept her lashes lowered. When her legs threatened to collapse, she offered a throaty plea.

"Luke!"

He answered by scooping her into his arms and carrying her back to his room. When he gently deposited her on the bed, her eyes fluttered open. The sharply etched lines of tension around his mouth and eyes made her pulse skitter erratically, and his heavy-lidded eyes seared her with more heat.

"I'll take a quick shower and be right back," he told her with a promise in his voice.

Susan was too dazed to protest. She was still trying to catch her breath and regain her equilibrium. He'd literally swept her off her feet, and tossed her into a whirlpool of eroticism. She fought to regain some control of her spinning senses.

The sound of the shower in the adjoining bathroom brought her eyes more fully open. The room had only one small lamp lit, casting the room in shadows. It was a masculine, no-frills sort of room, but she liked it.

The bed, Luke's bed, their bed, she reminded herself, was king-sized and carved from heavy oak. The décor was a mixture of black and maroon. The patterned bedspread had been tossed aside and Susan was lying on clean, fresh sheets.

She felt exposed again, and shifted her legs restlessly, creating a slide of silk against cotton. Her body was still tingling from Luke's touch and every movement set her senses whirling again. She pressed her hands over her breasts to relieve the continued ache, but it didn't help. She wasn't sure what would help, yet she instinctively knew that he could make it better if she allowed him.

Trusting him with her body meant trusting him more than she'd ever trusted any other human being. The thought was daunting. Especially since she knew his desire was only founded in physical need.

When the shower shut off she was both anxious and panicked again. Then Luke came through the door and all conscious thought left her mind.

She could only feel. Feel the impact of the sight of his big body wrapped in nothing but a towel. He was using another towel to rub excess water off his hair, and the muscles in his arms flexed with the action. His chest was broad and covered with a whorl of golden hair that arrowed past the towel. His legs were long and muscled and strong.

His gaze was leveled on her as he tossed one towel aside and finger-combed his hair while moving toward the bed. Susan's heart was pounding with a suffocating rhythm, pumping overheated blood throughout her body. Her chest rose and fell and her nipples beaded again. When he loosened the towel from his waist, her gaze dropped. It found more golden curls and fully erect evidence of his aroused state.

Her breath scattered and her gaze flew to his. His features were tight with undisguised desire and she felt panic explode inside her. When he dropped his full weight on her, alarm bells started jangling in her head.

She wasn't ready for this! It was happening too fast and rapidly getting out of control. She wanted to slow down, to scream for him to stop, but Luke was already sealing her lips with his hard, hungry mouth.

Susan brought her hands up to force some distance between their locked torsos, but he was far too heavy to shift. He seemed unconcerned about control as he rocked his body against hers in ancient demand. She didn't part her thighs to accommodate him. He was suddenly too hard, too heavy, too impatient, and she was in full panic.

Images of another night intruded as her memory flashed back to the time Shane had come home drunk, woke her from a sound sleep and raped her. She'd nearly suffocated that night, too, gasping for breath but unable to draw air into her lungs.

She tried to jerk her head out of his grasp, but he held her securely. When Luke finally lifted his mouth from hers, she managed a choked cry.

"I can't breathe!"

He immediately shifted his weight, and she took advantage of the move by shoving him aside, rolling from beneath him and across the bed. She quickly rose to her feet and stood panting, her eyes locked with his.

"You're scaring the hell out of me!" she accused.

It took a few seconds for the passionate haze to clear from his eyes. Then his features twisted into the most bitter expression she'd ever seen.

"Is it harder to suffer my attentions than you expected?" he snapped, his words as sharp as her rejection. "I'm not pretty-boy Shane, but you probably thought you could forget that, didn't you?"

"It's not like that at all," she argued, trying to calm her racing heart. He thought she was comparing him to Shane, and she hated the very thought. She didn't want him to think he didn't measure up to her expectations. "You're just moving too fast."

"According to Shane," he snarled the name, "you like it that way. He got his kicks telling everybody how insatiable you were."

Susan felt as though he'd slapped her, the blow slamming against her with a staggering force. Had he believed all Shane's lies? The little fantasy world she'd created this evening was destroyed and reality chilled her to the bone. She actually felt the color drain from her face.

When she finally found her voice, it was heavy with bitterness. "So you thought by marrying me you'd get your land, a quality broodmare and an insatiable bed partner?" The thought made her feel exposed and vulnerable.

Pain laced her next words. "Well I'm sorry if you believed Shane, but all he told you was lies, bold-faced, deliberately concocted lies. Our marriage was nothing but a sham. The closest we ever got to sex was the night he raped me!"

Utter silence descended, broken only by the sound of their ragged breathing.

Luke fought the haze of passion and tried to make sense of her words. If she was lying she was a real pro, because her tone was scathing, her eyes were brilliant and she'd gone deathly pale. There was a brittle tension in every line of her body. He went still and tense as his mind battled with a barrage of conflicting thoughts.

"He raped you?"

"He scared me out of my mind, and for the first time since I met you, you just reminded me of him!" On that parting shot, she found strength in her legs to run out of the room, not bothering to shut the door or take time for more clothes.

She raced across the hall, down the stairs, along the first floor hallway and was struggling to unlock the garden door when Luke finally caught up with her. He wrapped both arms around her and stilled her progress. Susan turned, ready to fight him off, but was swiftly swallowed in a gentle embrace, her head pressed against his chest as he spoke to her in a quieting tone.

"Calm down. I'm not going to hurt you. Just stop trying to run from me."

Tired, shaken and short of breath, she abruptly stopped struggling and collapsed against his solid strength. He pulled her closer and her arms seemed to involuntarily slide around his waist. She wasn't really afraid of him, just hurt, confused and angry.

"Explain," he insisted roughly. "I can't make any sense of this unless you give me some details."

A shiver raced down her spine. She couldn't bear to tell him the truth about why she married Shane, but she realized that her new marriage didn't stand a chance unless she described the physical aspects of the old one. Still the words seemed to get locked in her throat.

"Shane forced you to have sex against your will?"

The concept of a woman being raped by her husband wasn't that unusual, but it contradicted everything he'd ever believed about her and Shane's relationship. If they hadn't been in love, or at least lusted after each other, why had they married in the first place?

"Why?" he prompted.

"Because we only pretended to marry for love, and he promised our marriage would never be consummated. He thought he could seduce me into changing my mind but he couldn't, so he decided to use force."

Pretended to marry for love? Nothing she said was making much sense, but Luke didn't question her honesty. He just tried to keep her talking. "What did you do?"

"When he finally passed out, I beat him with a baseball bat," she confessed. "It sounds cowardly, but no more than attacking a woman while she's sleeping."

An image of Shane a couple years ago, bruised and limping, flashed into Luke's mind. He'd claimed some thugs had attacked him outside a local bar.

"So why'd you stay with him?"

"Butch was living with us then, and I didn't want him to learn the truth."

"Weren't you afraid of Shane after that?"

"I told him I'd kill him if he ever touched me again, and I guess he believed me. We had separate bedrooms and he never stepped a foot in mine again. There were plenty of women willing to provide him with sex, so he just left me alone."

The feel of her warm, pliant body was clouding Luke's thinking. There was plenty they needed to sort out, but his top priority at the moment was their physical relationship. His tone was low and carefully controlled when he finally spoke.

"Let me get this clear. The only time you had sex with Shane was when he forced you? Was that the only time in the last three years?"

Susan didn't speak, but nodded in the affirmative.

"Why didn't you tell me any of that before we got to the bedroom stage?"

She didn't lift her head, just mumbled the words against his skin. "I was hoping I wouldn't have to," she confessed. "You wouldn't have believed me anyway."

She didn't want to do any more explaining. It would only lead to questions she couldn't or wouldn't answer. She was determined to put the past behind her and build a new life with Luke. Within the circle of his arms, desire began to stir to life again. He was still totally naked. His flesh was smooth and warm with tight chest curls that brushed her cheek. He smelled of soap and Luke.

Tilting her head, she found his eyes in the shadowed darkness, and then placed her fingertips on his lips. "This is supposed to be our night. Please don't let him steal another second of it."

She saw an instant of resistance to her plea, and then she watched him mentally change gears and will away the bad thoughts. He let out a pent-up breath and his eyes grew smoky again.

"Have you had some good experiences with sex?"

Heat suffused her body, but she held his gaze and gave him the truth. "No."

It was a long minute before he spoke, and she could tell he was having difficulty controlling his reaction to her denial. His body was swelling against hers and the feel of him brought renewed trembling to her limbs.

"And you don't think I needed to know that?" He finally asked in a thick, graveled tone.

"I thought maybe you wouldn't notice."

That had him muttering obscenities. His hands flexed convulsively at her waist. His voice, when he spoke again, was razor sharp.

"I didn't notice, and I could have hurt you bad."

Susan was aware of that particular fact, but she hadn't allowed herself to think much about it until she'd been trapped under his big, virile body.

"It doesn't have to be so traumatic, does it?"

The total innocence of the query rattled him even more. "How the hell should I know?"

The answer didn't reassure her, but his next actions and words did. He took a deep breath and lowered his head to nudge hers. He buried his face in her hair and whispered in her ear, enunciating very clearly.

"We can go more slowly."

He was willing to try again. Relief washed through her, and she gave him a fierce hug. She was embarrassed by her inexperience, but she didn't want him to give up on her or their marriage.

"You're sure?" she asked, easing some distance between them so that she could see him again.

Luke nodded his head. Maybe he was the worst kind of fool, but right now the ache in his loins was so painful and heavy that little else mattered.

"What if we can't get it right?" she asked in a barely audible tone.

Her question seemed to ease the tension a little. It teased a slow, incredibly sexy smile to his lips, making her heart flutter in renewed excitement.

"I guess we'll have to do like all the other married people do," he suggested solemnly.

A frown creased her forehead. "What's that?"

"Keep practicing until we get it right."

"Oh!" she gasped. Then he was sweeping her into his arms again and clutching her against his broad chest. She slid her arms around his neck and watched him in fascination as he retraced their steps to the bedroom.

This time when he laid her on the bed, he came down beside her. He leaned toward her with one arm propped above her head and the other across her stomach.

"We have a lot of talking to do, but it might help if we get past the physical hang-ups first."

Her eyes widened a little, watching him in wary fascination. She couldn't seem to stem the flow of blood to her cheeks, and the heat of his big body seared the rest of her. She desperately wanted to reach out and caress him, yet wasn't bold enough to do it. Luke wasn't the least bit shy about touching her. One hand began to play with her hair while the other hand slid over her ribs to her breasts.

He cupped first one and then the other, molding the soft mounds and teasing their tips until she moaned with pleasure. His gaze stayed tangled with hers for a long time. It dropped to where his fingers had roused her nipples to rigid points. She watched his eyes cloud with desire as they skimmed over his handiwork and then lifted to hers again.

"Would you like to have my mouth on your breasts?" he asked in a low, husky query.

She closed her eyes to shield her vulnerability. She'd probably just die if he expected her to be able to verbally express everything she wanted and needed at the moment. She, herself, didn't understand.

When she didn't immediately respond, he coaxed, "Susy?" He used a nickname she hadn't heard for years. "Tell me what you want, so we don't make any more mistakes. Okay?"

"Okay." The word was little more than a sigh.

"Is it all right if I take off your gown and kiss your breasts?"

"Yes." Oh God, yes, she thought.

He slid one slim strap off her left shoulder, ran his fingers across her throat and then slid the other strap out of his way to peel the silk down to her waist.

Susan's heart was doing somersaults in her chest and she began to wonder if his fast, furious approach might not be easier to withstand than his slow, easy one.

Chapter Six

Luke's head came down and she caught her breath in anticipation, but he didn't take her nipple into his mouth as he'd done before. Instead, his tongue alternately bathed each tight bud with hot moisture, leaving them to dry in the relative chill of the air before repeating the action again and again.

Her fingers and toes curled. A new, slow-burning tension invaded her body and it was difficult to lie still. When she could no longer stand the teasing lap of his tongue she grasped a handful of his hair and urged him closer.

He didn't disappoint her. While one hand molded her right breast, his mouth locked onto the left, nearly making her wild. Waves of delicious sensation turned into spasms that arrowed from her breasts to her womb. She shifted restlessly on the bed, amazed at her body's responses.

"Luke!" she cried, suddenly impatient.

His mouth left her breasts and went on a hot foray across her neck to her throat, where he sucked on an erratically beating pulse.

When he'd kissed his way to her ear, he murmured, "We're taking it slow, remember?"

He was making her crazy, and she wasn't even sure how to satisfy the desperate yearning. For starters, she clutched his head with both hands and dragged it up to hers for a kiss. Their mouths met, his still patient, hers almost frantic. She parted her lips and immediately welcomed the thrust of his tongue. Luke shifted his weight more fully over her, rubbing his chest against her sensitized breasts.

She moaned into his mouth and wrapped her arms around his shoulders, pulling him closer as she slowly undulated her body beneath the strength of his. Their tongues dueled, and then she sucked greedily at his until she drew a groan from deep in his chest.

He drew back, his eyes on fire, his breathing harsh. "You're not playing fair," he charged. "Kisses like that make a man lose his head."

Susan took the criticism to heart and forced herself to calm down. He was trying to stay in control, and she'd been urging him to lose it. Her only defense was his ability to completely shatter her control.

"You haven't told me everything you like yet," he declared as he slid down her body and recaptured a nipple with his mouth, sucking deeply. After giving equal attention to the other breast he slid lower, easing the gown down her body as his mouth discovered new territory. Her stomach muscles clenched as she felt a shower of kisses across her abdomen. She gasped as he continued to explore the soft flesh of her thighs.

Susan was sure she would hyperventilate at any minute. It was becoming more and more difficult to draw air into her lungs as his mouth continued to discover ultrasensitive flesh. Her body was taut and quaking with explosive tension she prayed he knew how to relieve.

He gave her a brief respite as he pulled back to toss her gown aside, and then his hands and mouth went back to work at driving her insane with need. When his fingers began to knead the delicate flesh at the cradle of her thighs she nearly came off the bed.

"Luke!" she cried, throwing her head back against the pillows as he stroked her to a frenzy of need. Her hands were clenched into fists at her sides and the strength of his caresses brought her hips off the mattress.

Then he was sliding his full weight over hers, but this time her only distress stemmed from not being able to drag him close enough. She clutched at his shoulders and clung to him with all her might.

They were both soaked with sweat, their breath coming and going in harsh pants. Their eyes were glazed with a passionate fever as they met and locked. Luke nudged her thighs apart and settled between them.

"I'll be gentle with you," he whispered roughly, "but I can't promise it won't hurt."

She was beyond caring until he tried to complete their union. Pain and panic invaded her along with his big, powerful body. She tensed, alarm filling her eyes as her muscles reflexively fought the intrusion.

"Easy, it'll be all right," he swore gruffly, battling to gently but firmly penetrate her unyielding flesh.

Susan wasn't as sure. She'd gone from pliant to tense in an instant. His tension was just as fierce. The effort he was making to control his desire was evident in every sharp line of his face. She forced herself to lie still and stop resisting.

Then Luke wrapped his arms around her and reversed their positions, bringing her on top of him with their bodies still straining to become one.

Her eyes lit with surprise, but she felt infinitely more comfortable and in control. After a few additional seconds to adjust to the feel of him, she felt a resurgence of desire. This time it seized her with twice the force and ten times more primitive need for satisfaction.

Her already flushed features caught fire as Luke's hungry gaze trapped her own. She felt wanton, yet wildly uninhibited for the first time in her life. She felt in control and took control of their loving.

Her gaze never left his tight features as she began to rock her hips against the turgid strength of him. Her earlier cravings were nothing compared to what she experienced now, and the tempo of her movements increased in a frenzied rush until her control shattered and the satisfaction she'd been seeking suddenly radiated within her.

She cried out, shocking herself with the ragged sound of her cries. Then she felt a final, violent upward thrust of his body, and she collapsed against him in exhaustion.

For a long time after all they could do was fight for air into deprived lungs. Susan knew she was dead weight on his chest, but she couldn't have moved if her life depended on it.

She was enthralled by the whole experience he'd given her. The lifetime wait had been worth the reward. She felt closer to him than she'd ever felt to another human being. Neither of them had confessed their love, but instinct told her that Luke couldn't have made such beautiful love to her without feeling some emotion.

She knew men were different from women, and that the emotional aspects of loving weren't always as important to them, but she still didn't believe he could be so patient and tender if he didn't care a little. It was enough to spark more hope for their future.

"I'm sorry if I'm too heavy," she finally managed, her face still pressed to his heaving chest. The apology came without an effort to correct the problem.

Luke was stroking her hair with one hand and had the other locked around her waist. He started to speak, but had to clear the huskiness from his throat first.

"You're not heavy."

"That was incredible," she whispered back almost reverently.

There was a wealth of satisfaction in his voice when he responded. "Liked it, huh?"

Her only response was a nod of her head. She hadn't just liked it, she'd loved it, the closeness, the passionate need, the strength of their responses to each other. She loved being so close to him. It was one area of their relationship where they could become totally compatible. It wasn't all she yearned for, but maybe the intimacy would spill over into other aspects of their lives.

A sudden concern leapt to her mind. What if Luke had been so worried about pleasing her that he hadn't enjoyed it himself? He was a lot more experienced. What if she rated really low by comparison? She hadn't done anything to please him. She'd only wallowed in his attentions.

Lifting her head, she sought his eyes. They were closed, but opened and lit with curiosity at her probing stare.

"Was it all right for you?" She had to ask, even though voicing the question brought a rush of heat to her face.

A big, lazy smile spread across his face. He looked well satisfied, but she desperately needed reassurance. He seemed aware of the fact.

"It was good," he insisted.

"You're not just saying that?"

In response, he rocked his hips against hers, making her gasp as she felt him pulse within her. While their eyes were locked, he slowly turned her in his arms until he was on top.

"It was so good, I want more," he declared, his eyes going dark as she wriggled beneath him.

"Oh!" was all she could say before his mouth trapped hers and passion escalated again.

A long time later, when Susan was fast asleep, Luke propped his arms behind his head and stared at the ceiling. Replays of the evening kept running through his head, making sleep impossible. How much of what Susan had told him could he believe? He'd thought her tale about Shane raping her was an elaborate ploy until he'd tried to penetrate the virginal tightness of her body. Damn! Just the memory brought him to swift, aching arousal again.

Could she have faked the innocence? The tightness sure as hell hadn't been faked. She'd been wet and wanting and more

Becky Barker

than ready for him. She should have sheathed him easily, yet she'd had trouble. Was she just naturally small, her muscles naturally tight, or was there a way women could control such things?

Shane had called her insatiable. Would the six months of celibacy since his death make a difference? He didn't know and he sure as hell couldn't ask anybody.

She'd played him for a fool when she'd married Shane, and he wasn't likely to forgive and forget. He didn't know what kind of game she was playing, but he knew she was hiding something.

Right now all he cared about was keeping his family's land intact, having a responsive woman to warm his bed and having a wife who was willing to bear his children. He trusted Susan to satisfy those needs.

And he did want her physically. That he couldn't deny, even to himself. He'd wanted her for years. She'd become a fever in his blood that had scalded him all the time she'd been married to his cousin.

He'd learned to control the need, to reinforce it with his disgust at her duplicity. He had little respect for women who so easily switched their loyalties, but he didn't intend to let it happen again. She was his now. If she was insatiable, he'd make sure she never have reason to complain. He could be insatiable, too.

Like right now. Tonight. With her soft, warm body pressed against his and the intoxicating scent of her filling his nostrils, it was hard to think of anything but sating himself again. He shifted his legs on the bed as he fought the heavy pull of desire.

She'd been so eager and responsive, yet seemed so unsure and inexperienced. He refused to trust her or even his own instincts. She was temptation, and he was sorely tempted to wake her again. He ached too much to sleep, but he'd had plenty of experience with that particular ache. He could and would control it.

* * * * *

The sun was high by the time Susan awoke on Saturday. The night had been long and filled with incredible discoveries, giving her a whole new perspective on life and love.

Considering the lateness of the hour, she wasn't surprised to find herself alone in bed. She missed Luke, but knew he had a busy day. Tonight was John's birthday party, so he and everyone else on the ranch would be preparing for the big barbecue and celebration.

She felt a moment's guilt at not being up at the crack of dawn to help, but then she remembered how she and Luke had greeted the dawn. A smile accompanied the memory.

He was awe-inspiring. He'd taught her things she'd never known about her own sensuality. He'd drawn a passion from within her that had amazed her. Together they'd scaled heights of pleasure beyond her wildest imaginings.

He hadn't seemed daunted by her inexperience, even though she had been at first. He'd been alternately patient and forceful, teaching her a broad spectrum of responses. His stamina was amazing.

She stretched, her body tingling with sensitivity as the sheet slid over her tender skin. A blush crept up her neck and face as she remembered how thoroughly Luke had caressed and explored her body. She wouldn't have believed it possible to be so uninhibited, yet there was no denying her responses to his loving. He might be her first and only lover, but she was wise enough to know that all men didn't make love so unselfishly. Luke was anything but selfish.

The bedroom door opened, startling her, and she jerked the sheet up to her chin. The man on her mind entered, closed the door and then leaned against it while staring at her.

She gave him a tentative smile, and he returned it with a sexy masculine one. His gaze seemed all-seeing as it lingered on her disheveled state. Her hair was a wild tangle, her skin still pink from a long night of his caresses, and she was totally naked under the sheet.

Susan felt her senses stirring in response to his blatantly sexual perusal. "Good morning," she offered, to break the tension humming between them.

He quietly corrected her. "Good afternoon."

She dropped her eyes. "Is it very late?"

"Late enough that Rosa wanted to come and make sure I hadn't done you bodily harm last night."

More heat invaded her cheeks as she realized the whole ranch staff would be speculating. "I can't believe I slept so long. I feel totally decadent."

"You're under doctor's orders to rest, remember?"

There was an unholy gleam in his eyes as he teased her. She responded to it like a flower to the sun.

"Doctor Peters might be a little shocked at your method of relaxing me."

Luke's gaze sharpened and his tone took a serious edge. "Were you shocked?"

Susan dipped her head, focusing her eyes on the sheet. She knew he didn't want a flippant answer. He was asking if their night of loving had unsettled her. Did that mean he had accepted the truth about her and Shane?

"I was shocked but pleased," she said.

"What was shocking?"

She searched for the best explanation. "I just never imagined it could be that way."

Luke moved to the bed. His knee dropped beside her and she tilted toward him as his weight pressed down on the mattress. He cupped her head in his hands, turning her face to him. His tone took on the now-familiar sexiness of arousal.

"I imagined it, but the reality was even more incredible," he admitted.

Then his mouth was devouring hers as if to remind her of how easily he could make her want him. She returned his kiss with fervor, wrapping her arms around his broad shoulders. His big, hard body inflamed her senses. The feel and taste and scent of him stirred longings she'd barely had time to develop.

Several long minutes later, he slowly withdrew from the kiss. Her lashes swept up, and she stared at him with her heart in her eyes. She wanted to tell him how much she loved him, but didn't want him to confuse the feelings with desire. She had plenty of both, but he probably wouldn't believe it.

"If you keep looking at me like that, I'll never let you out of this bed," he threatened.

"So?" she dared.

He groaned and rose to his feet, causing the sheet to slide to her waist. Before she could snatch it back up, one of his big hands cupped and caressed a bared breast. His thumb skimmed a nipple.

Her breath caught in her throat, and she placed her hand over his. "If you keep doing that, I'll never want to get out of this bed."

Luke chuckled, a wickedly pleased sound that made her heart swell with happiness. He gave her nipple a tiny pinch and then pulled the sheet up to her neck.

She grinned at him. "Rosa's going to think you've locked me in the bedroom. She'll be up here to free me soon."

"She's worried that you haven't had anything to eat and you might be starving to death," he explained, moving a few steps to the door. He turned back to her, leaning his right shoulder against the frame. While crossing his arms over his chest, he fastened his gaze on her again.

His stance was casual, and she couldn't help but admire the sleek, beautiful lines of his body. He wore his usual attire of snug, worn jeans and a T-shirt that hugged his chest and arms. A sudden mental image of all that masculine beauty in the nude brought a rush of longing so intense she shuddered.

It suddenly occurred to her that most newlyweds felt the same. That's why they needed extended honeymoons. They just couldn't bear to be parted. He was still within a few feet of her and yet she missed him.

She knew her eyes were full of hungry need as they met his. His flared in recognition of the hunger, but she swiftly redirected her attention. "Now that you mention it, food does sound pretty good."

He didn't comment on her provocative body language. "Rosa made sandwiches and told the men to fend for themselves, but she'll probably make an exception for you."

She didn't want special attention from the housekeeper. "I imagine she's busy."

The reminder of party plans dampened her good mood. She wasn't ready to face so many people. All she wanted to do was spend time with him. She didn't want to be the center of everyone's attention or have to start dodging personal questions. The subject of her marriage to two Hanchart men would be of unbearable interest.

"We still have to talk," he reminded, eyes narrowing.

Panic surged through her. Now that he knew a few of the details about her relationship with Shane, he wanted to know why she'd married his cousin. He'd asked her several times during the night, but she'd managed to put off explaining.

She couldn't get by with it much longer, yet she dreaded the pain and humiliation the truth would bring. She didn't want the ugliness to mar the sweetness of what they'd found together.

"But not right now?" She pleaded for more time.

His expression hardened. "You can trust me with your body, but not your secrets?" he ground out.

"It's not like that," she countered.

"Do you think it's going to hurt my feelings? Did you marry him just because he got the good looks and the charm? Because he was everybody's idea of the perfect catch?"

"No!" She'd never been drawn to Shane physically or emotionally. She'd never preferred him over Luke, but her new husband wouldn't believe that without knowing all the details. Maybe not even then.

"Do you really think I'm that shallow?" she asked, dropping her eyes to where her fingers nervously plucked at the sheet.

He didn't answer, and she dared a glance at him. She could tell by the tightening of his mouth that he didn't like her defensive question any more than she liked his. He was closing up again, shutting her out and destroying the intimacy they'd created throughout the night.

"Why does it matter so much? Why does it have to affect us?" she beseeched. "Can't we just let it go?"

"It's a fact. You married him." His tone was hard. "That's not going to change, and believe me, nobody's going to let us forget it."

"If I had the power to change it, I would," she insisted, eyes wide and pleading. "But I don't. It was a mistake. We were all wrong for each other and we made a horrible, regrettable mistake."

"Then why did you do it in the first place?" he demanded, straightening from his relaxed position and glaring at her with suddenly hostile eyes. "What made you think you could make it work if neither of you really wanted it?"

When she gave no response, he continued, "If you fancied him, why didn't you have a real marriage? Did he scare you? Was he a sexual pervert of some kind?"

Susan looked him straight in the eyes. "I was not in love with him, and I didn't care about his sexual preferences as long as he stayed away from me."

She flinched when the declaration seemed to make him more angry. It was impossible to comprehend her marriage to Shane without knowing all the details. She understood his frustration, and knew she'd have to confess the truth to him soon.

"Please, Luke. Just give us a little more time."

"Us?" he growled.

"Just us. Without Shane's ugliness."

His retort held more anger and frustration. "You can't just wish it away."

"I know." She couldn't put him off much longer, but she wanted to pretend they were a normal, happy couple. At least for a few more hours.

"I promise I'll explain everything tomorrow. Just let me get through this party tonight."

She wanted another night in his arms too, another night to help cement their relationship before he learned the whole ugly truth.

His eyes bored into hers, searching for secrets. Finding only entreaty, he abruptly changed the subject. "I've got to get back downstairs and help set things up."

Susan breathed a sigh at the reprieve. She hated his contempt and mistrust, but not as much as the idea of disclosing the truth.

"I'll take a quick shower and come help."

"You know we're going to catch hell from the family, don't you?" He added another worry. "Especially since Granddad was the only one who was invited to the ceremony."

"Will they have to know we had a party with the ranch staff?" That would add insult to injury.

"There's no keeping secrets around here. Granddad already had a call from Linda. She's on the warpath."

Susan gnawed her lip. "Will she make a scene?"

"Probably not in front of half the community, but there are lots of mean, subtle ways to show displeasure. She knows 'em all."

He was right. Linda would have condemned their plans from the beginning and done everything in her power to thwart them. Now she'd be furious because they hadn't included her. It was a no-win situation.

"She'll just have to get over it." She'd let Shane's sister intimidate her before, but not any longer.

"Just remember that she can't hurt you if you don't let her. You're my wife now. If she causes trouble, she answers to me." On that, he turned and left the room.

Susan fell back against the pillows and pulled the sheet over her head. The desire to shut out the rest of the world was strong. She just wanted Luke, and wished their relationship wasn't so complex. For at least the millionth time she wished she'd never met Shane Hanchart.

She could have gone to Luke as soon as Shane started blackmailing her, but she'd been too scared and humiliated. Her first concern at that point had been protecting her brother. He'd been so young and vulnerable and confused.

He had been all the family she'd had left, and she would have done anything to protect him. It had been her responsibility to care for him. As the elder, she'd had more time to develop self-worth and emotional security. Butch had so little of both.

Looking back, she knew she hadn't really helped her brother by marrying Shane. She'd only compounded his feelings of guilt and inadequacy. The decisions she'd made had been the wrong ones. That was obvious now.

Butch had died when his motorcycle crashed into a tree, but she'd never been certain the wreck was an accident. He'd been so depressed and had been drinking heavily. Nothing she did ever seemed to help. His death would burden her conscience for the rest of her life.

Doctor Peters had counseled her at the time, telling her that Butch needed to learn to cope with his problems. He'd explained that lots of young people her brother's age faced even worse situations than the death of their parents.

Spoiling Butch had done more harm than good, but she hadn't known how else to protect him. Every time she'd tried to lecture him, he'd looked so forlorn and bereft she couldn't stand it.

She'd let him get away with skipping school, driving too fast, staying out too late. There had been a couple skirmishes with the sheriff for curfew, then Butch had turned eighteen and become a legal adult. The problems had gotten worse until finally one became blackmail material.

Thoughts of her brother always made Susan painfully sad, so she tried not to dwell on the past. Now Luke was insisting that she relive it all with explanations. It made her feel bereft too.

There was a chance the truth would cost her his tentative trust. She knew one night of loving couldn't erase all the heartache they'd suffered, but it was a new beginning.

She hoped she'd gained a little respect from him last night. He couldn't help but notice how inept and inexperienced she was, refuting Shane's claims about her sexual appetites. If Luke realized he was her first and only lover, maybe it would put a dent in the armor around his heart.

He had plenty of experience with women, of that she was certain. The knowledge brought a stab of jealousy but it was tempered with common sense. His experience could benefit her too. She wanted him to know how special he was to her. She wanted him to be the one who taught her everything there was to learn about loving. She wanted all his faith, love and trust, she thought, burrowing her head into the pillow.

Unfortunately those were things that had to be earned. She couldn't expect his unconditional acceptance if she wasn't willing to trust him with the truth.

Maybe she could solve the problem with most of the truth. She'd already told him she and Shane weren't lovers, so why did he need to know about the blackmail? It would only make things worse. Maybe she could get by with a partial explanation for the whole family and keep her horrible secret.

They'd all be here tonight. Shane's sister, Linda, and her husband, Dan Tarken, lived closest and had two children, Molly, age ten, and Alex, six. Their chunk of Hanchart property was within ten miles of the main ranch, so they were the most frequent visitors.

Their brother Brad and his wife, Lynette, had two young daughters—Tami, five, and Paige, three. Brad ranched another Hanchart property a hundred miles further south, closer to Lynette's family. They reserved their visits to holidays and special occasions.

Shane's mother, Bernice, had remarried and moved to the East Coast after the death of their father. She visited occasionally, but didn't get involved with family affairs.

Although Luke was the oldest of the Hanchart grandchildren at age thirty, Linda was only a year younger. Brad was a couple years behind her and Shane had been the baby. For all intents and purposes, Linda reigned as matriarch of what was left of the family.

Susan wasn't looking forward to seeing her sister-in-law. While the other woman had never been openly hostile, she'd made it clear she didn't approve of a marriage between her beloved younger brother and an orphaned woman with no family wealth or social standing.

During the two years of her marriage to Shane, Susan had never done anything to endear herself to his family. She'd attended very few get-togethers because Luke's cold contempt had stung even though she deserved it.

Seeing him with other women had hurt as well, so she hadn't been very sociable. It was mostly her own fault Linda resented her, she mused. Now she had to find a way to bridge the gap caused by her own indifference because they were Luke's family too.

Her thoughts drifted over various ways of explaining her motivations without causing even more scandal, and then she drifted back to sleep.

* * * * *

The next time Susan woke, it was to the sound of the shower running in the adjoining bathroom. She sat straight up in bed and glanced toward the window. It had to be late afternoon. A glance at the clock on the dresser confirmed the fact. It was after five o'clock.

Dear heaven, she'd slept the whole day! What would everyone think? It sure wasn't the best way to make an impression on her new ranch family, she thought, shoving her hair back from her face.

There was a tray of food on the bedside stand, and she checked out the contents. Luke was obviously in the shower and she was starving. She helped herself to a sandwich, some fruit and a glass of milk. It was still cool, so she guessed it hadn't been in the room long.

The shower shut off just as she was placing the empty tray back on the stand. She jumped out of bed and grabbed a cotton robe to cover herself before he returned to the bedroom. It was embarrassing enough to have slept all day, she didn't want him to find her still naked in bed.

Her hair was a mess. She was standing in front of the dressing table mirror trying to brush it into some order when he opened the bathroom door. One look at him had her hand pausing in midair.

Heat rushed through her body at his sheer masculine beauty. Wearing only white briefs, there was a lot of naked male flesh revealed. Her fingers curled on the urge to stroke his broad chest and ridged stomach, to feel the length of him pressed against her.

Her intense, uninhibited perusal and the admiration in her gaze had a significant affect on his big body. She watched in fascination as his arousal became evident and the hard column of flesh strained against the confines of his underwear. Her pulse became erratic, eyes flying to his in amazement.

"You didn't know you could excite a man with just a sultry look?" he asked.

His tone was a mixture of arrogance and annoyance. Susan couldn't tell if he was annoyed with her or just the circumstances. Did he resent the effect she had on him or was he as easily aroused by other women too?

She frowned. "I guess I never thought about it much at all."

She watched as he closed his eyes and turned his back on her. She might be naïve in some ways but instinct told her he was fighting a surge of desire that he deeply resented.

His battle for control fascinated her even more than his swift arousal. Their reactions to each other were remarkable, and she wanted more time to explore him.

"We have to get through this damned party," he insisted, echoing her thoughts. They couldn't be alone again until much later.

Susan took his cue and refocused her attention. Grabbing clean underwear from her drawer, she asked, "What time will people start arriving?"

"The family will be probably be here around six. Granddad and everyone else, after seven."

"When are you planning to announce our news?"

Luke started pulling on khaki pants. "Linda has already spread the word, but I'd still like to discuss it with the family first. Then Granddad wants to announce it later to everyone else."

He pulled on a short-sleeved knit shirt and tugged it into place. Susan continued to stare at him. The white of the shirt accented the golden bronze of his skin, giving him a masculine appeal that could steal a woman's breath.

Her sudden silence and riveted attention caught his. "You have a problem with what I'm wearing?"

The defensiveness of his tone startled her, making her eyes go wide and curious. He'd mentioned Shane's good looks on several occasions. Was it possible that he thought himself less attractive than his cousin?

"You have to know how gorgeous you are," she admonished, blushing wildly.

The laugh he barked held no humor. "If I've suddenly become gorgeous, you must really be taken with the sex."

His rebuff of her shy compliment hurt and she reacted with anger, snapping back at him. "Do you really think women prefer pretty-boy handsome to men with soul-deep, sexy eyes and features with real character? If you do, then don't lump me with anyone that simple-minded," she grumbled, her voice rising.

He'd hit a nerve by mentioning her newly discovered fascination with sex, so she lambasted him for that too. "I know what I like, and if it's sex related it's only because you have a body to die for. And I'm sure I'm not the only woman who ever told you so."

Her little tirade brought more hot color to her cheeks. She realized, belatedly, how possessive she sounded, but she was already dreading sharing him this evening with old girlfriends and ex-lovers. There were bound to be some at the party.

Luke had gone very still, his eyes narrowing as her agitation increased. Susan turned abruptly, fled to the bathroom and slammed the door behind her.

Then she leaned against it and drew in a deep, steadying breath while dragging her hands through her hair. Dear God, what had gotten into her?

She was sounding like a shrew after less than twenty-four hours of marriage. She couldn't believe she'd actually yelled at him. He'd think he married a lunatic. Nerves. It was just the tension, she decided. Her nerves were strung tight and she was almost sick with worry over the ten-day wonder their marriage would cause. She just wanted it behind her. She'd apologize for the loss of composure. Later. When they could be alone again and say to hell with the rest of the world.

After a few minutes she heard Luke leave the bedroom and managed to get herself into the shower. The spray stung some of the areas that had received the abundance of his attentions last night, sending a new wave of desire over her.

For a woman who'd had very few sensual thoughts in the past, she was making up for it in spades today. She had to get her act together.

It took less than an hour for her to bathe, shampoo, dry and curl her hair, then get dressed for the coming evening. The outfit she chose included a dress from her college days. It was a deep turquoise that looked good with her fair hair and light tan. Neither too dressy nor too casual, it seemed perfect for the party.

Her mother had thought it too short and tight back then, but her loss of weight made a difference. Now the soft cotton and A-line style just skimmed her figure, enhancing but not hugging too tightly.

The dress had a scooped neckline with a rolled collar that folded into narrow straps on her shoulders. Susan added a small gold chain around her neck and a matching gold bracelet adorned her wrist.

Her hair hung heavily to her shoulders and the ends were curled to add body. She wanted to avoid her usual scraped-back look, but wasn't used to having it around her face. As a compromise, she slid gold-toned combs into each side of her hair to pull it above her ears and was satisfied with the results.

It had been so long since she'd worn makeup that she was a little hesitant, applying it sparingly. A touch of eye shadow, mascara and lip gloss. Blusher wasn't necessary. She was sure she'd have a natural blush most of the evening, either from embarrassment, frustration or anger.

The heavy sense of dread didn't lighten, even when she knew she was looking her best. Mentally chiding herself, she reasoned that the night wasn't going to be over until it had begun. There was no use stalling any longer. It was half past six already.

A pair of strappy high-heeled sandals matched the dress, but Susan decided not to wear them. She'd be on her feet all night and wasn't used to the heels. A pair of flat sandals would have to do. She slipped her feet into the shoes and headed downstairs.

Luke was coming up the hallway as she reached the bottom of the stairs. He halted at the sight of her. Every muscle and nerve in his body leapt to life, reacting to her femininity, loveliness and the innate sensuality he hadn't had nearly enough time to explore.

The physical reactions irritated him. It was one thing to desire her in his bed, but altogether different to be bombarded with cravings every time she was near. She looked shy and unsure of herself. Whether it was real or faked, it brought out protective instincts he didn't want to feel.

He'd felt the same way after her parents died. He'd felt the same wild, inexplicable cravings coupled with an intense desire to protect her. Look where those emotions had gotten him.

Susan's heart raced when he stared without saying anything. The tightness of his expression made her uneasy. "Is this all right?" she asked self-consciously, running her hands down the sides of the dress.

His eyes smoldered for an instant, and then became hooded. His tone was clipped. "You'll do fine."

She grimaced inwardly. He was still annoyed with her, or he didn't feel like wasting words on compliments. Her morale could have used a boost.

"The family's all in my office."

Well, that was enough to make any man frown, she supposed. "I'm sorry I wasn't down here to greet them."

"It doesn't matter," he assured her, pulling one of her hands through his arm to escort her down the hall. "It's better to face them with a united front."

Her stomach was churning and she suddenly wished she hadn't eaten anything.

He sensed her increased tension. "Just remember you're my wife now," he reminded. "You don't need their approval. If anybody offends you tell them to go to hell."

Easy for him to say, she thought. He was used to being the ruler of the roost. He'd proven his ability to be in charge of the family's vast holdings and wealth. He'd earned respect in the family and community with hard work, dependability, intelligence and strength.

She'd yet to prove herself worthy of him. She didn't want their marriage to incorporate blind acceptance. She wanted to earn it.

When Luke swung the door of his office open, he ushered her inside and slid an arm around her waist. She welcomed the gesture when conversation ceased in the room and everyone turned toward them.

Linda was as beautiful as ever in a blue silk pantsuit. With fair complexion, hair and eyes, she and Shane had looked so alike that people sometimes mistook them for twins despite their difference in age.

Her beauty was somewhat marred by the resentment in her pale green eyes. "Nice of you to join us."

Luke started to speak, but Susan interrupted a reprimand that was certain to start a full-scale battle.

"Hello, Linda," she replied calmly. "I apologize for keeping everyone waiting."

Next she greeted Dan, a tall, thin, attractive man with dark hair and eyes who was normally congenial unless his wife was upset. As a banker and pillar of the community, he was as socially conscious as Linda.

She greeted Brad and Lynette by name, then added, "It's nice to see you all."

"We hear you have some news." Brad cut to the heart of the matter. He was her favorite of Luke's cousins, almost an outcast on his own side of the family because he'd never allowed Linda to control him.

"Susan and I were married last night," Luke explained without expression. "We didn't invite anyone because we wanted to keep it simple and uncomplicated."

"From the sound of it you had quite a celebration," interjected Linda. "You might have given us some advance warning so that we didn't have to learn of it through gossip."

"Granddad stood up for me, and Rosa for Susan," Luke continued. "You know Rosa can't do anything without making a party of it and feeding people."

"Well, we can at least add our congratulations," declared Lynette, moving toward them. A slender, dark-eyed brunette, she was often a mediator for family disagreements.

"I wish you all the best of luck," she added, giving them both a hug. They returned her hugs with sincerely felt thank-yous.

"I second that," said Brad, offering a hand to Luke. The two men were a lot alike in size and coloring, except for their eyes. Brad's were green, like the others on his side of the family.

He hugged Susan and she gave him a warm smile. Then the other couple stepped aside.

Linda offered no congratulations, and her husband followed her lead. "I guess the two of you think you've made a good match, but I think you'll live to regret your hasty marriage," she warned them.

The circumstances created by Shane's will were no secret to the family or the community, so everyone would know the marriage was one of convenience. There was no sense trying to refute the truth. Susan regretted the fact, but couldn't change it, so she didn't comment.

When no one else spoke, Linda's eyes welled with tears. "Shane's barely been dead six months. I don't know why he left things the way he did, but certainly you could have waited a more respectable length before remarrying. What will people say?"

"They'll say the same thing they said when Susan lost her parents and then her brother," supplied Luke, his tone and expression uncompromising. "They'll say she has to get on with her own life."

The pronouncement effectively put an end to verbal complaints, but Linda's eyes were still misty and accusing. Susan couldn't help but feel sorry for her. Regardless of her own feelings for Shane, she knew his sister had adored him, had been stunned by his will and was still trying to cope with his loss.

"Shane wasn't the type who'd appreciate a long mourning period," Lynette offered. "He enjoyed life to the fullest and wanted everyone else to, too. I'm sure everyone will understand that no disrespect was intended."

Susan threw Lynette a smile of gratitude for coming to their defense without hurting Linda's feelings even more.

"There may be a few single ladies and their hopeful mothers who get ticked off because Luke finally married," Brad teased, trying to lighten the mood. "But I figure they'll get over it."

Luke gave him a grin and then glanced at Susan. Her brows were furrowed at the mention of other women.

"Have you told Caroline?" asked Linda, relishing another angle of attack against her cousin.

Caroline Adkens was Linda's best friend. She and Luke had dated occasionally. She'd made no secret of the fact she wanted him for husband number three.

"I had no reason to tell her," he stated flatly. "If she comes tonight, she'll hear about it along with everyone else."

Susan's eyes were troubled as they darted between Linda and Luke. She knew he'd dated Caroline in the past, but Linda made it sound as though they had an ongoing relationship. Just how close were they now? Were they lovers?

Luke's tone and words denied any sense of obligation toward the other woman, but Susan wondered if Caroline felt the same. Would she try to make trouble? Worse yet, would she try to persuade him he'd made a mistake?

Before anything else could be said, a knock at the door announced four impatient youngsters who didn't like being excluded from the adult conversation. With an invitation from Luke, they poured into the room and demanded hugs and kisses.

Brad's two preschoolers were dark-haired pixies who adored their cousin Luke. They both vied for his attention and were simultaneously scooped into his arms. They planted noisy kisses on his cheeks and began talking a mile a minute.

Susan watched his face soften and his eyes warm with affection. Her chest constricted at his gentleness. He was such a good man. He'd hate being called sweet, yet he had a soft spot for children and animals. Probably because they were so vulnerable and he was so strong.

Watching him with Tami and Paige made her all the more aware of his gentle, caring nature. He was endlessly patient with them and would make a wonderful father. A wave of love washed over her, making her heart ache with longing. She silently prayed she could give him children of his own.

She wasn't aware that everyone else in the room was watching her watch Luke until she finally shifted her gaze and encountered four other watchful pairs of eyes.

Was she wearing her heart on her sleeve? Did she look like a lovesick bride? The idea flustered her, making her more self-conscious. Then she reminded herself that it was important they know her true feelings.

"Did you really marry Luke?" asked Molly, a thin, sensitive ten year old who was a pale shadow of her mother.

Susan smiled and hugged the impressionable child. "Yes, I really married Luke."

"Are you still my aunt?" she asked with a serious tone and expression.

"Absolutely," Susan reassured.

"I would have been a bridesmaid," declared Molly. "My friend Tonya was a bridesmaid once, and she taught me everything she had to do."

Linda quietly scolded her daughter, but Susan wrapped an arm around her slender shoulders in support. "If we'd had a big wedding, I would have been honored to have you as a bridesmaid. But we decided to have a very small ceremony."

"Did you have a maid of honor?"

"Rosa was my matron of honor."

Molly's eyes widened in alarm. "Oh no, I forgot to tell everyone that Rosa said the guests are arriving."

General laughter followed her belated announcement.

"Then we better head outside," said Luke, swinging Tami and Paige to the floor. They dashed to their parents and everyone headed out of the room.

Luke grasped Susan's arm, but she gently disengaged it. "Go ahead," she explained. "I'll be out in a minute." He looked ready to argue, but decided against it and joined the exodus from the room.

Susan caught Linda's eye before she could leave. "May I have a minute?" she asked.

Linda and Dan exchanged glances. She nodded, and he followed the others from the room, leaving the two of them alone.

"I know our decision to marry is a hard one for you to accept," Susan began when it was quiet again, "But Luke and I are committed to making our marriage work."

Linda's temper flared. "You were married to Shane for two years, and I never once saw you look at him the way you looked at Luke just now," she charged, her eyes filling with more angry tears. "If it's Luke you love, then why did you marry Shane and deprive him of real love and happiness the last years of his life?"

Susan could never tell her the whole truth, but she decided on a carefully disguised version.

"I know this will be hard to believe since Shane did everything he could to keep the truth from people, but our marriage was strictly one of convenience."

Linda gasped as if she'd been slapped. "How dare you say that? It's a lie or Shane would have told me. He told me everything."

"It's not a lie." At least not entirey, Susan mentally corrected, then braced herself for Linda's reaction to her next statement.

"Shane asked me to marry him because John was threatening to cut him out of his will if he didn't settle down."

"That's not so!" Linda charged, but her tone was less vehement.

"I know you loved him, Linda, but you weren't totally blind to his faults. He drank too much and threw far too many wild parties."

The older woman didn't dispute the facts. "So you decided to get married?" Her tone was disbelieving. "He just said 'let's get married' and you agreed?"

"I was desperate for a home and some security for Butch," Susan managed without choking on the part of the explanation that was a total lie. "Shane and I came to an agreement. I took care of the cooking and housekeeping, and he kept a roof over our heads."

"That's it?" the older woman exclaimed. "You just sold yourself for the price of a home? How could you sleep with a man you didn't love? Was the attraction purely physical or was it just for the Hanchart name?"

Susan flinched, but couldn't deny the accusation without telling the truth. Her private life was none of Linda's business, yet she owed it to Luke to explain.

"Shane and I were never in love, and we were never lovers."

Linda's eyes and mouth opened wide in astonishment. "You expect me to believe that? I knew my brother better than anyone else in the world. I saw the way he was with you, he was a devoted husband."

"You saw what Shane wanted you to see," Susan countered. "You loved him and everyone wanted him to be happily married, so he pretended he was."

"And I'm to believe he either lived as a celibate in a loveless marriage, or that he found someone else to satisfy his needs and was an adulterer? That takes a lot of nerve, especially since he can no longer defend himself."

Susan's tone hardened. "You can accept what I've told you or not, but for the sake of the family, you might give it some thought."

"And I suppose you think this little chat will just make everything better," was Linda's haughty reply.

Her arrogance finally snapped Susan's calm. "The only person I care about is Luke. I'm promising if you do or say anything to humiliate, hurt or malign him, I'll never forgive you, and you'll live to regret it."

"You dare to threaten me?" Linda asked, instantly furious.

The door to the office was shoved inward and John entered the room, startling them both into silence.

"Ladies," he nodded. "I slipped in the side door to avoid the crowd gathering out back. I thought I'd mention that your voices are starting to carry." The censure in his tone had them both blushing.

"Our family isn't nearly as big as it once was," he continued. "There's only a few of us left, so I'm expecting the two of you to work out your differences."

"Did you hear the cock-and-bull story she's trying to feed me?" asked a petulant Linda.

"I heard part of it," he said. "I thought there was something strange about Shane getting married so soon after I threatened to disinherit him, but I'd hoped it was for the best."

Linda went pale and stared at John as if he'd grown an extra head. "You actually threatened to disown him?"

John nodded. "That much of Susan's story I can vouch for," he assured her.

"How could you?"

"You know he was spoiled and headstrong," John reminded. "Don't make him a martyr in death. If he hadn't married and settled down, he'd have paid a higher price for his wild lifestyle."

Linda didn't respond. Her expression hardened and she gave them a terse "excuse me" before exiting the room, leaving John and Susan to stare after her with equally troubled expressions.

"Sometimes Linda's pretty full of herself, the family power and wealth," he explained, turning his attention to her. His eyes, so much like Luke's, pierced her with steely intensity.

"She could easily be convinced you married Shane for the family's wealth and social standing. Much as I hate to contradict your story, I don't believe it."

Susan sighed and gave him a slight smile. His words both worried and warmed her. She didn't want him insisting on answers, yet his faith in her personal integrity was heartening. She knew he wanted to hear the truth but she couldn't give it to him.

When she didn't respond he continued, "Have you told Luke the same story you just gave Linda?"

She looked him directly in the eyes. "Luke's a little too much like his grandfather," she explained wryly. "I doubt he'd believe it either."

"And you don't want to tell him the real truth?"

"I'd rather cut off my tongue."

He was momentarily startled by her vehemence, and then he threw back his head and roared with laughter. Susan relaxed a little and smiled at the happy sound.

"Oh, that's rich," John managed when his amusement lessened. "Well I guess I'll have to leave it to you young 'uns to work out. Just take some advice from an old man, don't leave it too long. It'll just fester."

He offered his arm. "I'm late for a surprise party."

"You're the guest of honor, you're supposed to be late," she teased, tucking her hand through the crook of his elbow. "How else can you be surprised?"

John grumbled that his ears were too old to tolerate people shrieking and that he never had cared for stupid gag gifts. As they made their way through the house, the sound of the crowd grew louder. Susan separated herself from him in the kitchen where Rosa was still busily preparing food.

"It's about time you two showed up," said the housekeeper. She gave Susan a thorough once-over and decided she was unharmed by her wedding night or her initiation into the family fold.

"Susan, could you please take this plate of meat out to Juan at the barbecue? Linda's ready to make a little birthday speech, John, if you're ready to hear it."

"Ready as ever," he grumbled.

The women exchanged a grin as he went out the door, looking as though he was throwing himself to the wolves. His appearance sent up a cheer from their guests.

"He really loves these parties," Rosa whispered. "He'd die before admitting it, but I know he looks forward to it every year."

Susan picked up a plate of meat. "I'm sure he does," she agreed, but she certainly wasn't looking forward to it.

Chapter Seven

❧

Susan unconsciously straightened her shoulders and lifted her chin as she stepped out of the house onto the patio. Colored banners and balloons were strung all over the backyard and pool area, adding to the gaiety of the beautiful summer evening. A throng of people stood around laughing, talking and sipping cold beverages. As expected, half the community was in attendance.

It was still hot, but the sun's heat would soon be waning and they might get lucky enough to have a cool evening breeze. By dark, dozens of carefully strung lanterns would be lit to add a golden glow to the celebration.

Her eyes searched for Luke and found him talking with a group of men. They were local ranchers who belonged to the Cattlemen's Association. He was past-president and a highly respected member. He was also a good friend and neighbor.

Luke had been watching for her, and his gut tightened the instant she stepped into view. Resentment flared along with his body's urgent response, and then he wrote it off as a natural reaction after a night of passion. Especially a night of passion that had been preceded by too many months of celibacy.

The evidence of Susan's physical discomfort had kept him from satiating himself with her, but it was just as well. He needed to keep a tight rein on his control where she was concerned. He wanted to know what had transpired between his wife and his cousin. Had Linda intimidated Susan? Their gazes met, the question flashing between them, but her expression was carefully bland.

He watched as she made her way to the barbecue, smiling and greeting people on the way. She looked more confident than she had earlier, and he wondered if she was feeling smug about retaining the Hanchart name and all the perks that went with it. Had she privately taunted Linda with the knowledge or had the two of them spent more time discussing Shane?

"If I were a few years younger, I'd have to come a courtin' that one," said Pete Rudger, a longtime friend of John's.

Luke felt a jolt of annoyance when he realized that the men he was standing with were all watching him watch Susan. He didn't appreciate their speculative glances, but didn't blame them for their curiosity.

"Found any way to get around that clause in Shane's will?" asked Pete, airing the subject that had been the talk of the community since the news hit the grapevine.

"You're not gonna let old Matthews win this battle, are you?" asked another rancher.

"Yes and no." Luke responded to their questions in order without elaborating. They'd all know the details soon enough, so he pointedly changed the subject.

Meanwhile, Susan was making her way around the patio greeting guests. She knew most everyone, had known them all her life, yet didn't feel she knew anyone well. These last few years she'd done her best to fade into the background. That suited her just fine, but she owed it to Luke to make an effort at socializing.

After a short while, she turned her attention to a portable stage that had been set up for the band. Linda was tapping a microphone to quiet the crowd and garner attention.

She was a gracious hostess as she welcomed everyone and thanked them for coming to help celebrate John's birthday. No one would ever guess that she'd been in a temper and tears just minutes ago Susan had to admire her for her charm and composure.

Linda and her granddad shared a few teasing remarks, and then she turned the microphone over to him.

John repeated the welcome and thanks. "I guess if y'all enjoy the parties enough, I'll have to keep having birthdays," he teased. "I'm figurin' on livin' 'til about a hundred."

The declaration was greeted with a rousing cheer, laughter and applause. Susan scanned the crowd for Luke again, but couldn't find him. Then she felt the warmth of his touch at her back.

He stepped beside her, keeping a hand on the back of her waist, sending heat spiraling through her body. She turned her head to him and smiled, feeling less isolated with him close. It seemed impossible that she'd become so addicted to his solid presence in so few hours.

"I have a special announcement to make this evening," John was saying. "It's my duty as the patriarch of the family and my great pleasure as a proud granddad to announce Luke's marriage."

A collective gasp went through the crowd, with all eyes searching for the man in question.

"Luke and Susan were married right here at the house last night," he continued. "With Reverend Thompson doing the honors. I'd like to wish the newlyweds a long and happy future. And maybe even mention my desire for a few more great-grandchildren."

More laughter erupted and after only a brief hesitation, Luke and Susan were bombarded with congratulations. She noted a great deal of speculation in their guests' eyes, but tried not to be unnerved by it.

There were the expected comments. "We had no idea you were even dating!"

"Well, aren't you the secretive ones?"

"When did all this come about?"

"Why didn't you let anyone know?"

"You should have told us, we'd have thrown a party."

Some of the congratulations were genuinely sincere and Susan appreciated them. She was hugged and kissed and patted on the arm and back. Other people, mostly women, weren't so pleasant. One dared to remark that she obviously hadn't been a merry widow. Luke quickly showed his disfavor with a sharp retort that served as a warning to anyone else who might make crude comments about Susan.

For all intents and purposes the announcement went over well, but being the center of attention was still a strain. John seemed to sense when they'd had enough and loudly declared that it was time to eat. The bulk of the crowd shifted toward food-laden tables.

Caroline Adkens approached when the crowd surrounding them thinned. The other woman was a tall, shapely redhead wearing a yellow shorts outfit that showcased her long legs. Although not classically beautiful, she was very attractive with an aura of raw sensuality that appealed to men.

It didn't appeal to Susan. She stiffened, mentally preparing for more malicious feminine digs, but Caroline wasn't interested in her. Her eyes locked on Luke. Then she gave him a congratulatory hug and managed to press her breasts against his chest for an indecent amount of time.

Susan was ready to peel the woman off, when Luke did it himself. He grasped her shoulders and gently but firmly set her aside. Caroline's eyes flashed with satisfaction, as though she was certain the feel of her body had the power to disturb him.

Susan fumed at the thought. He didn't appear overly affected by the other woman, but was he? He was a deeply sensual man. He'd left no doubt in her mind about that. Maybe that's why Caroline had appealed to him in the first place.

With that thought came a surge of red-hot jealousy that was so intense it alarmed her. She'd never been the jealous type. She didn't want to be any more dependent on him than she already was. Nor did she want to be bombarded by emotional reactions as passionate as jealousy.

A glance at Luke quickly jolted her back to reality. His eyes were cool and watchful, the arrogant tilt of his brow mocking her reaction. Susan realized that her expression was tight with distaste and she made a concerted effort to relax.

Luke turned his attention back to Caroline. "You'd better get something to eat before it's gone," he told her, his dismissal doing nothing to smooth their guest's ruffled feathers.

"I think I'll hit the bar first," she said. "I can really get into a party mood once I've had some of your private stock bourbon."

The comment was heavy with innuendo, suggesting that she was very familiar with Luke's preferences, and that he was partial to her party mood.

Susan cringed at the thought. "Witch," she muttered under her breath.

Luke threw her a sideways glance. "Did you say you're hungry?" he asked, dropping a hand to her waist and guiding her toward the tables.

He leaned his head close to her ear. "Forget about Caroline and Linda. Eat and keep up your strength," he advised. "It might be another long night."

Susan blushed, knowing that was the reaction he'd hoped to spur but helpless to contain it. Heat coursed through her at the reminder of how they'd spent the previous night and of another one to come. She didn't know if she could stand the anticipation.

For the next couple of hours she renewed old friendships. She'd lost contact with many other classmates when she'd gone to college and been married to Shane.

Luke stayed close to her for most of the evening, but when they got separated he usually made his way back to her in a short while. Susan assumed he was playing the part of dutiful bridegroom.

Even though everyone present was bound to speculate about their reason for marrying, he apparently wanted to make it clear that the marriage was going to be more than a business arrangement.

That was fine with her. She liked having him near and feeling his touch. Whether it was a guiding hand at the small of her back or a brief touch on the arm, he generated warmth and a sense of security she hadn't even realized she needed. Whenever and wherever he touched her, her skin tingled with pleasure.

She was a little more hesitant about touching him, but the contact their bodies made was a sweet, torturous reminder of the passion that simmered between them. By the time the sun had set she was growing increasingly anxious to have the party over. She was craving his sole attention.

A four-piece band had been hired to play music. They began to tune their instruments when the lanterns were lit. A small space in front of the stage had been cleared but no one seemed anxious to be the first on the floor.

Caroline sauntered up to the stage and blew into the microphone a few times to test it. She laughed and teased the band members, drawing chuckles. She'd obviously managed to get herself in a party mood. Luke was close enough for Susan to feel him go tense and she glanced at him.

"What's she up to?"

The two of them had gradually shifted into a corner of the patio that wasn't too crowded. People were clustered everywhere, but none too close. They could actually talk with some privacy.

At first she didn't think Luke was going to respond then he explained, "She has this thing about dancing. She made such a big deal of it that I stopped asking her out."

"You think she's going to ask you to dance?" Susan wondered. A little public humiliation? The woman scorned?

Luke flashed her a tight smile for perception. "I wouldn't put anything past her."

Susan remembered Shane making some derogatory remarks about Luke not being able to dance. It was unusual in this area where barn and school dances were some of the rare forms of entertainment, but that didn't mean everyone had to enjoy it.

She had always loved music and dancing even though she was out of practice. Caroline was temporarily forgotten as she concentrated on Luke. Being a man with such natural athleticism and coordination, she couldn't imagine him not being a good dancer if he'd give it a try.

"Why don't you dance?"

"I just don't," he grumbled, his tone suggesting it was a sore subject.

"I would have thought you'd like it," she said, sipping her cola but shifting her gaze back to Caroline.

The suggestive tone of her voice drew his full attention. He shifted closer, drawing her gaze back to him.

"Why would you think I'd like it?"

"It's a lot like making love," she supplied, her voice a throaty whisper as she shyly flirted with him over the rim of her glass.

"You think?" he drawled in a low tone, intrigued. "I never quite saw it that way."

"You press your bodies together, hold on tight and slide around the floor," she insisted a little breathlessly. "It's all a matter of coordination and rhythm."

A glimmer of interest lit his eyes and his voice dropped to a whisper. "And you think I'm good at that, huh?"

Every nerve in her body shivered in reaction. "Real good," she assured.

"So what's your suggestion?"

Encouraged by his continued interest, she said, "Well, you're very good at one, and I'm pretty good at the other." The rest came out in a rush. "We could compare notes."

"You're offering to teach me a few things?" he asked, brow raised.

Susan shrugged her shoulders and lowered her lashes, flirting as she hadn't done in years. Then Caroline commanded their attention again.

"It's time to dance, partygoers," she announced. "I know all you cowboys are a little shy about being the first one on the floor, so I think our new bride and groom should get things started. It's a tradition, you know."

Although well on her way to being intoxicated, the other woman was still sober enough to know exactly what she was doing. She threw a "gotcha" look at Luke.

An expectant hush was followed by a general murmur of agreement while everyone searched out the newlyweds again. Those who knew Luke never danced understood Caroline's little trick, but the others just thought it a nice gesture.

Susan heard his low curse and understood his frustration. She didn't want to let Caroline win this little skirmish. Emboldened by her success at flirting, she snared his eyes again and practiced a little seductive persuasion.

"I can't promise it won't hurt," she repeated the words he'd whispered to her last night as they'd made love, blushing despite the bold ploy. "But if you want to give it a try, I'll be gentle with you."

Luke's eyes flared with the swift brilliance of the flame of a match. The look he gave her was hot enough to start a fire deep in the pit of her belly and shoot sparks over the rest of her. He took the glass from her suddenly shaky fingers and set it aside. With a possessive hand at her waist, he ushered her to the dance floor amidst cheers from the guests.

The look on Caroline's face was incredulous and outraged, but Susan didn't witness it. She was too fascinated with Luke and the feel of his hard, warm body as he pulled her into his arms.

"Just press our bodies together?" he asked, his tone gone low.

His left hand enveloped her right one and Susan slid her other hand over his shoulder until their bodies were pressed snugly together. The breath hissed out of her as she felt the strength of his arousal against her stomach.

"See what you get for playing with fire?" he taunted, eyes dark and gleaming. "You didn't leave me any choice but to dance."

The heat raging through her made it hard to catch her breath, but she finally managed a soft laugh and some bold teasing. "Hiding behind the little lady's skirt?"

"It would seem," he agreed, though the supreme confidence in his tone outweighed any signs of weakness.

Her eyes stayed glued to the brilliance of his as she continued to challenge him with sensual promise. She was suddenly high on life and the heat in his eyes.

It had been so long since she'd had the desire or confidence to flirt or reason to feel good about herself. She credited Luke for the good feelings. He was the best thing that had ever happened to her, and she just wished she had the courage to tell him so.

His gaze skimmed her face and then focused on her mouth. For just an instant his eyes glittered with a hunger so raw that it scattered Susan's breath. Her chest constricted, and her hold on him tightened convulsively. Her heart stopped and then restarted with a surge of overheated blood through her veins.

Other couples gradually joined them on the tiny dance floor, but nobody cut in or interrupted them while their bodies swayed in time to the music. Their dancing was little more than a shuffle of feet but she was so conscious of his hard body that everything else faded in importance.

Normally a very reserved person, her reaction to Luke temporarily destroyed her inhibitions. For once, she didn't try to hide her emotions. Instead she gazed at him with wide, awestruck eyes. Those who watched were speculative. Some cynically regarded it as an act, some thought it was very special and others hoped it wouldn't last.

As the evening passed the majority of their guests wished them well, at least to their faces. Most stayed until well after midnight and then they began leaving in large numbers. The adult members of the family thanked them for attending and bade them good night.

Brad, Lynette and their girls were spending the night, so Tami and Paige had already been put to bed. Dan and Linda had allowed their children to stay up late, but both were battling heavy eyes.

Luke helped Dan carry Molly and Alex to their car while the other men folded chairs and tables then carried them to the barn for storage. Linda, Susan, Lynette and Caroline helped Rosa with a final cleanup of the kitchen.

Then Susan went onto the patio to do a final check for dirty dishes and Caroline followed in the pretense of helping. The other woman wasn't too drunk to corner her with some spiteful comments.

"You needn't feel too smug about talking Luke into marriage you know," she said conversationally. "Everyone knows he and his granddad would do just about anything to keep the Hanchart heritage intact."

If she expected to get a rise out of Susan, she was disappointed. She knew exactly why Luke had married her. What she wondered was if he'd ever considered marrying Caroline.

"Luke's a law unto himself," was her only comment.

"Oh, he's independent enough," Caroline agreed. "But your mother was one of Alma's dearest friends and you know John adored her. When your mother died so soon after Alma,

John took it upon himself to gather you into the family fold one way or the other."

"John was very kind after my parents' deaths, but he's a kind man," said Susan. Caroline was piquing her curiosity, yet she didn't want to give her the satisfaction of realizing it.

"Didn't you ever think it was a little strange that Luke suddenly came courting?"

While Susan collected trash and disposed of it, the other woman leaned against a table, lit a cigarette and took a deep drag before she continued.

"He started seeing you because John asked him to. I think he even would have married you to please his granddad, then the next thing he knew you were married to his cousin. It must be especially grating to feel obliged to marry you now since he refused to date any of Shane's castoffs after Lori Pagent."

Lori Pagent? Susan vaguely remembered the name from high school, but Lori had been closer to Luke's age than hers. She had married and moved out of state a few years back. What did she have to do with anything?

Caroline explained, "Lori was Luke's first and only real love until she got the hots for Shane. She tried to keep seeing them both, but then Luke found out she was screwing around with his cousin.

"Lori realized too late that Shane wasn't the Hanchart with the money or control, so she dumped him and went running back to Luke. But it was too late. By then he'd vowed to never have anything to do with any woman who found Shane attractive."

The little speech was punctuated by puffs of smoke and ended with a malicious laugh. Susan was appalled by the story, yet tried not to react. If it was true, it explained more of the rivalry between the cousins, and maybe why Shane had gone to such extremes to get even with Luke.

"Yes, indeed," Caroline drawled. "I bet it really sticks in Luke's craw that he had to marry you for the property, especially with all his friends suggesting he's settling for Shane's leavings. It's enough to make a proud man sick to death."

Her little lecture was cut short by Luke's return. He glanced from one to the other, the taut line of his jaw tightening even more.

He didn't need a psychic to tell him Caroline had been trying to cause trouble. At this point he was fed up with people in general and troublemakers in particular. He'd just suffered a tantrum from Linda, a host of sly congratulations from fellow ranchers and more than enough snide comments to last a lifetime. He was fed up.

"Dan and Linda are ready to leave," he told Caroline, keeping a tight rein on his temper. She'd had too much to drink and shouldn't drive. "They'll take you home and one of the ranch staff will bring your car tomorrow morning."

"You're welcome to take me home," she suggested throatily. "You know the way well enough."

"So does Dan," he clipped. Too little sleep and too much tension had him as irritable as hell. He wasn't in any mood for games.

She gave him a smoldering look and conceded defeat. "Well, I guess I'll be running along then," she said as she sauntered toward the door. She ran a hand up his arm as she went past. "Thanks for everything, sugar."

Susan gritted her teeth to keep a civil tongue in her head. She wanted to tell her to keep her hands to herself. The parting shot made her feel like smashing things. She took out her frustration on the trash.

Luke started toward her, but then everyone seemed to converge on the patio again. Juan and a couple of the ranch hands returned from carrying troughs back to the barn. Brad, Lynette and John came back from seeing off guests, and Rosa came out of the kitchen.

"That's it for tonight," the housekeeper declared with satisfaction. "Time to go home."

"I'll second that," put in John. "Thanks for the party everyone. I'll see you tomorrow. I promised the youngsters we'd have a picnic if they behaved tonight, so we have a picnic to plan."

Brad turned to Luke and Susan. "Would you mind if Lynette and I walk Granddad home? The girls should stay asleep and we won't be long."

"No problem," they chorused.

Everyone departed with final good nights, and Luke turned to Susan. Tension radiated from him, making her wonder if it was sexual in nature or if someone had made a parting remark that roused his temper.

"Go on upstairs. I'll do one last check down here and be up when Brad and Lynette get back," he said.

Her gaze scoured his features. She wanted to ask him what was wrong, but couldn't find the courage. "I'll take a quick peek at the girls."

She started past him to the door, their bodies brushing as each moved at the same time. Luke's arm shot out to steady her. One touch was all it took to ignite the passion that had simmered beneath the surface all night. She wasn't sure who made the next move, but she was suddenly clutched close to his unyielding hardness.

He dragged her closer, the angry stiffness of his body suggesting he couldn't resist, but resented the loss of control. Then her arms locked around his neck as their mouths met in a punishing rush.

Whatever anger and frustration he felt swiftly erupted into savage hunger. Hours of wanting and needing and waiting, of being close and touching, yet forced to control their needs finally exploded into a kiss that was deep and hard and hungry. His mouth ground onto hers and she met it with equal fervor.

Her grip on his neck tightened and when his tongue plunged into her mouth she rocked her body against his in answering need. A shudder rippled over him as she pressed herself closer to the rock-hard length of him. The kiss went on and on and on, tongues stroking and entwining until they were both dizzy with wanting. Susan's body came alive, and all the sensitive places Luke had explored last night began to throb with renewed excitement. His kisses seduced, and she was ready and willing to succumb.

When they finally dragged their mouths apart to draw in air, their breathing was so rough it hurt. His eyes seared her with silvery heat, their faces so close that it was hard to tell whose breath they breathed.

His voice was a ragged sound. "You'd better go."

"I guess," she whispered without conviction. Then she sank all her fingers in the thick silk of his hair and tugged his mouth to hers again.

The second kiss was less desperate, but no less arousing. They took turns sucking each other's tongues until they were sharing moans and were breathless again.

When their lips next parted, he lifted her against his body and carried her through the kitchen door, down the hall and to the bottom of the stairs. Then he set her down and gave her one more swift, hard kiss.

"I'll be up as soon as I shut off lights and lock doors," he said.

Her throat was tight, making her beyond words. She nodded and turned to climb the stairs without looking back even though she felt the heat of his eyes watch her every step of the way.

Once upstairs she drew in a deep, calming breath and went to the guest room to check on Tami and Paige. The little girls were sharing one big bed with a host of stuffed animals. They looked so precious that it made her breath catch again.

The need for a child of her own was intense and her heart ached with longing. It suddenly occurred to her that she and Luke hadn't used any form of protection last night. She could already be carrying his child. Her hand involuntarily moved to her stomach, and she remembered Caroline's suggestion that Luke only married her to supply heirs for the family. It was partly true, yet she didn't think his passion would be so fierce if he didn't care a little.

She didn't want to consider the fact that he could be as passionate with any woman. Nor did she want to think about Lori Pagent. But the doubts came anyway.

Had Luke and Shane both been wildly in love with her? Was she the reason they'd been such rivals in everything? The reason Shane had blackmailed her into marriage and then lorded it over Luke every chance he got?

The ranch and the property were part of the reason, but she'd always thought there had to be more. If Caroline could be believed, the whole affair would explain a lot of things she hadn't understood before now.

Unfortunately, it also made her realize just how difficult it must have been for Luke to marry her. Would he ever be able to forgive her? She could better understand his resentment and anger, but she didn't have a clue as to how she could overcome such resentment.

Was he still carrying a torch for Lori? The idea brought almost suffocating pain. She couldn't bear to think about it.

Had people taunted him in private tonight? Could that account for the almost angry passion they'd just experienced?

Regardless of what had happened in the past, they had the future to worry about now. She sincerely hoped Caroline was wrong about people suggesting that Luke had settled for Shane's leavings. What a crude thing to say. Would his friends and neighbors be so cruel?

She'd never loved Shane. Luke might not trust her enough to believe that, but it was the truth. Had Lori told him a similar story? He obviously hadn't believed her or he'd resented her affair with Shane too much to forgive her.

And then she'd done exactly the same thing, but without realizing it She'd dated Luke, married Shane and now was married to Luke. What a mess! What an incredible mess they'd made of ther lives.

It was up to her to correct past mistakes. The only way she knew to do that was to tell Luke the whole truth and confess her love to hm. She wasn't sure she had enough courage but if the alternative was Luke's unhappiness she'd find the strength.

Chapter Eight

இ

When Susan entered the master bedroom, she was a little surprised to find the bed made. She'd tidied the room before going downstairs, but hadn't taken time to strip the dirty sheets. Now the bed was made up with fresh linens.

A blush stole up her cheeks. Rosa must have found time to come and check the bedroom. Although the housekeeper normally did the cleaning, it was embarrassing to have anyone handling their rumpled sheets. It seemed such a private thing, so she made a mental note to let her know she'd take care of their room in the future.

Remembering the way Luke had made love to her last night, Susan decided on a quick shower. She grabbed the nightgown she'd worn for only a few minutes of her wedding night and headed for the bathroom. Once there, she slipped out of her clothes and pinned her hair atop her head. After adjusting the faucets, she climbed into the shower stall.

When she was nearly finished, she heard the bathroom door open and saw him silhouetted against the curtain. The breath was stolen from her as she watched him strip his clothes too. A violent quivering began deep inside her when he pulled back the curtain just far enough to join her.

Their gazes collided, rekindling the fire that had been tamped but smoldering all day and evening. Heat flared, singeing them both. Then Luke's broad back deflected the spray of water while his darkened gaze made a slow, thorough sweep of her naked, glistening body.

Her breasts swelled, nipples tightening as his eyes touched them just before his big hands came up to cup them. His thumbs teased both peaks to hardness.

"So responsive," he said in a tone rough with masculine satisfaction. "So soft and yet so hard for me."

His touch sent a pulsing riot of sensation from her breasts to her womb. Her heart pounded in a cadence heavy with desire.

"Closer," he commanded gruffly.

She swiftly took the step that brought their lower bodies into hard contact. She grasped his waist with her hands, both to steady herself and bring him closer. The feel of his hard, demanding flesh made her knees go weak.

She arched her hips against him and they both moaned as soft, water-slick flesh met hot, hard flesh. His arms enveloped her as he drew her closer and buried his face in the curve of her shoulder. His mouth sucked the sensitive skin of her neck as he gruffly whispered more words of arousal.

"I can't wait any longer," he growled roughly, sliding his hands to her hips, parting her thighs and lifting her against him.

Susan clung to his neck while wrapping her legs around his hips. She cried out as he entered her, but from joy rather than pain.

"Hold on," he rumbled as he clutched her tightly and sank into her welcoming warmth.

She needed him this way too, needed to be one with him, needed to feel the pounding force of his desire deep within her. She clung tightly to his broad shoulders as the strength and speed of his thrusts threatened to destroy their precarious balance. Then he was erupting, his big body quivering violently with satisfaction.

"Luke!" she cried his name as he trembled and shook in the aftermath of passion.

He rested his forehead against hers as he dragged her closer, clinging to her wet, quivering body until they could both breathe again. Susan thought he was cursing, but the roar of her own pulse made it impossible to be sure.

Long minutes later, when they'd recovered enough to step apart, he amazed her by taking the soap in his hands and bathing her. His gaze trapped hers while his long, work-roughened fingers cleansed and caressed her most sensitive flesh with gentle care.

Her breathing became ragged and her legs threatened to collapse, so she shoved his hands aside and returned the favor. Her soap-slick hands caressed the rippling muscles of his chest and followed the swirling hair on his belly down to the juncture of his thighs. A low moan escaped him as her touch brought him to rigid arousal. The water grew cool, but they were aflame again.

Luke's patience snapped first. He shut off the shower, wrapped her in a big towel and carried her to bed. Then he took a deep breath, reined his passion and began arousing her in every way he knew. The next few hours were spent in a sensual haze as his hands, mouth and body explored all the feminine territory he hadn't had time to pleasure the night before.

They slept a few hours, and then awakened before dawn to make love again. This time when he joined their bodies, she cried out the secret she could no longer deny.

"I love you!"

Luke reacted swiftly and fiercely, grasping her head between his hands and glaring at her with dark, turbulent eyes. "No," he growled in sudden anger. "No lies between us. What you love is the way I make you feel. What we have is lust. I don't want lies about love."

His words lanced her heart with agony and tears welled in her eyes. They seemed to intensify his anger but she couldn't stop them. He ground his mouth against hers and swallowed her tiny sob.

She arched her hips beneath him and returned his angry kiss. If he didn't want her love she could at least give him all the loving he needed until time brought some semblance of trust.

This time when they found sexual satisfaction, some of the sweetness was gone. His anger destroyed any chance of an intimate aftermath to their loving. Luke rolled away from her and Susan was devastated. All she could think to do was grab the sheet and cover herself protectively.

She'd never told any man she loved him, had never loved anyone the way she did him. She understood his reluctance to believe her, but it still hurt to have him throw the declaration of love back in her face. The pain was sharp, the wound deep.

After a few minutes, their breathing had regulated and they regained some control. It was obvious that neither of them would sleep again. The sky was brightening as Susan mulled over what she needed to say. She wanted his trust, so she needed to be completely honest. It was the only way.

"I think it's time I explained why I married Shane," she said, shattering the weighty silence of the room with her husky admission.

She felt the immediate renewed tension in his body. His gaze sought hers but she couldn't maintain the contact. Her gaze wandered to the window and she clutched the sheet like a lifeline.

"I told Linda that Shane and I had a business agreement. That he needed to prove to John that he could settle down, and I needed a home for Butch and me."

"She believed that?"

Susan shook her head slightly. "I don't know what she believed, but John verified the fact that he was ready to disinherit Shane if he didn't settle down. It gave Linda food for thought."

"But it's not the truth." His tone was flat.

"No," she confessed, and then mustered all her courage. "Shane blackmailed me into marrying him."

The rest came out in a rush as she blurted the truth. "He had proof that Butch was one of the vandals who terrorized your horses and caused the stallion to fracture his leg. He said he'd take it to the sheriff and make sure Butch was arrested if I didn't marry him and help pacify his granddad."

There was a wealth of contempt in Luke's next question. "And you let Shane get away with blackmail?"

Susan sat up and turned toward him, pulling the sheet around her. Her expression beseeched him to understand.

"How could I not? Butch was eighteen and would have been tried as an adult. You know Shane wouldn't have hesitated to follow through with his threats. He didn't have a compassionate bone in his body!"

Their gazes remained locked as he questioned her. "And you couldn't let Butch accept responsibility for his own actions?"

Susan paled, her lashes dropping as she fought tears. "I know now that it was the wrong thing to do. Wrong for Butch. Protecting him destroyed what little self-esteem he had. He hated us both for the mess we made."

Her voice quivered as she fought the black memories and dealt with the suffocating pressure of regret. Luke shifted in bed and for a moment she thought he would take her in his arms. Instead he rose and headed for the bathroom.

She drew in a deep breath, fought for control and then opened her eyes in time to see him reenter the room. He'd pulled on his jeans and found her bathrobe.

"Put this on and come downstairs with me."

Her glistening eyes searched his but found no trace of emotion. She accepted the robe and slipped out of bed. When she had it wrapped around her and secured they headed downstairs.

The house was quiet and lit only by the dim light of dawn. It would be a while before anyone else awoke. Rosa didn't work on Sundays, and the others would sleep late. He led her to his office, closed the door behind them and switched on the overhead light. He motioned for her to take a seat. Then he went to the wall safe, unlocked the combination and removed a videocassette tape.

Susan gasped and cried out. Panic spurred her to action and she went flying across the room.

"No! He swore on his deathbed!" she insisted, nearly frantic. "He said there weren't any other copies and I burned the original myself!"

She tried to snatch the video from Luke but he held it out of reach and restrained her with one arm around her waist. His tone was grim.

"Apparently Shane wasn't the only one with a copy. Rod Matthews had one too. He sent it to me after I fired him."

Another harsh gasp escaped her and nausea rolled in her stomach. Her eyes were wide with shock as she realized her mistake in trusting anything Shane said. He'd wanted a final guarantee that she'd never be accepted as Luke's wife.

"You've watched it?" she managed in a raw tone.

"At first, I figured it was some sort of X-rated film of you and Shane," he explained, his jaw clenching. "I planned to destroy it until you told me about the rape. Then I decided I'd better see what else Shane and Rod had been up to."

She pulled away from him and turned her back. Wrapping both her arms around her waist, she tried to still the violent churning in her stomach. The thought of Luke viewing the film hurt her unbearably. He shared her passionate love of horses and the damning evidence on tape left no doubt about the abuse his livestock had suffered.

No wonder he'd rejected her declaration of love. He already knew her ugly secret. He'd seen the crimes her brother had committed. She was too ashamed to even look at him. He was probably wishing he'd known about the tape before marrying her. Now it was too late to salvage the situation.

Damn Shane for lying! Damn him to hell for one more cruel, degrading trick. Explaining a crime spree to Luke would have been hard, but possible. Having him see it firsthand was altogether different. She'd only seen the video once, and it had made her physically ill.

If he'd had doubts about her social acceptability or her parenting skills, the tape would increase those doubts a hundredfold. He'd be appalled by her brother's actions as well as hers. She'd broken the law by withholding evidence in a criminal investigation.

The television clicked on and she heard Luke slip the tape into the VCR. Whirling, she made a lunge toward the TV.

"No!" she cried, trying to shove him out of the way. She fumbled with the buttons, but was able to push the pause before he pulled her away from the set.

"Let it play," he insisted tersely.

He held her firmly with one arm around her shoulders as he pushed the play button. The first sounds were those of glass being shattered and property being smashed.

"No!" whispered Susan as they watched familiar landmarks in the small town of Monroe being trashed by a car full of grown men. Windows were smashed, property destroyed with vicious abandon.

Drunken jokes and laughter filled in the time while the car made its way from Monroe to Hanchart property. Then there was the sound of wood splintering as fences met with destruction. But the worst was the panicked screams of innocent horses as they were chased around the pasture and terrorized.

Susan clasped her hands over her ears and buried her face in Luke's chest. A sob tore at her throat and he shifted to halt the video. She gasped, eyes widening as she felt the shudder that coursed over his body. An equally strong shudder racked her body and more nausea threatened.

"You know Shane planned the whole thing," Luke insisted. "He knew exactly what he was doing, what would infuriate me the most and shame you the most."

"Butch didn't know it was a setup."

"He was so stoned he didn't remember anything," he insisted. "The video was probably as much a shock to him as it was you."

She was shaking her head back and forth in denial. The lengths Shane had gone to with his deception were inconceivable to her. She pulled from his grip and turned toward the TV set.

"Watch it with me," he told her, rewinding and then replaying the worst scenes.

She took a deep breath and glued her gaze to the screen. Luke turned the volume up and her heart sank, but then she tried to distance herself from it like she would a fiction movie. Had Butch been the only one in a drunken stupor?

As she watched more carefully, the horror continued. The camera picked up the random acts of violence as the car full of men continued on a crime spree. They destroyed anything that happened to be in their path.

She tensed even more as she envisioned what came next. The sounds tore at her heart. They were those of Luke's prize horses, as the vandals' ruthlessness tormented them.

Susan slapped her hands over her ears again to block out the equine screams of fear and the sick, drunken laughter of the men in the car. It made bile rise in her throat.

"You need to pay close attention," he said, pulling her hands from her ears. "Take a good look at Butch."

For one long moment there was a closeup of her brother's face. He was seated in the passenger side of the front seat while the man in the backseat holding the camera zoomed in on him.

Luke stopped the video, rewound it and replayed that particular section again. Susan clasped a hand over her mouth to trap a sob as tears blinded her for an instant. The sight of her brother's boyish features made her sick with grief and a longing so intense that it hurt. Regardless of the situation, she drank in the sight of him.

"Take a good look at him, Susan," Luke demanded quietly. "He's almost comatose. My guess is that Shane made sure he was drunk out of his mind before they went on this little spree. Butch wasn't an active participant, just a pawn in Shane's ugly little game."

She swiped the tears from her eyes and tried to be objective. He was right. She saw more clearly now. Butch's eyes were glazed and the seat belt seemed the only thing keeping him upright.

"He swore he didn't remember any of it," she whispered in her brother's defense. "He was as shocked as I was when Shane showed us the video. Now I understand why."

There was no doubt about Butch's guilt in having been drunk out of his mind, yet he hadn't needed to suffer all the shame and humiliation Shane's scheme had caused. He was just another victim.

What had she done to her baby brother? Compounded Shane's crime by marrying him and adding to Butch's feelings of guilt and remorse? So much so that he couldn't bear to go on living? What a fool she'd been! And what a miserable, worthless guardian she'd been.

"Rod suggested that Shane was the director and cameraman on this project," said Luke as he shut off the television and returned the video to the safe.

Butch's face had been the only one clearly visible on the video. Two other men wore hats and their faces were kept in the shadows. The fourth man was never seen.

145

"I'd say the man in the dark hat is Matthews. If I'd watched this sooner, I'd have had him thrown in jail instead of just firing him."

Susan eased herself into a big leather chair and watched him pace around the room. Her thoughts and emotions were in total chaos. Her temperature kept swinging from the heat of humiliation to the chill of cold calculation. Mentally flaying herself for so many mistakes in judgment didn't lift the burden of guilt.

"Why?" Luke demanded, finally getting to the brunt of the matter. His steely gaze leveled on her after he settled on the edge of his desk.

Arms crossed over his chest, he continued to question her. "Why didn't you come to me with this? Why didn't you trust me more than Shane?"

Her eyes widened in shock. There was no way she could have gone to him at the time. She'd been too ashamed and guilt-ridden over what had happened to his livestock. His prize stallion had broken a leg and been put down. Others had been injured. He'd been absolutely furious, with good reason. There had been talk of little else for weeks.

The resulting investigation had left her in constant fear that Butch would be arrested. She'd had knowledge and evidence of the crimes, but had withheld it from the sheriff.

"Why?" he demanded again.

"I couldn't," she started.

"You preferred to marry Shane rather than come to me with the truth?" he ground out angrily.

"It wasn't like that," she tried to explain, but he cut her off.

"It seems pretty clear-cut to me," he snarled. "You thought you were martyring yourself for your brother, but all you were doing was falling in with Shane's plans. Maybe you really wanted to marry him all along."

"That's not true!" Susan exclaimed. "I never felt anything but contempt for Shane. Our marriage was nothing but a farce, a deliberate, calculated farce!"

"It seemed damned real to the rest of the world," he growled. "Maybe you were in on it too. Maybe you're the sort of woman who gets her kicks out of playing games with people's lives."

"That's totally unfair!" she snapped, jumping to her feet and glaring at him angrily. "You're twisting everything into lies, just like Shane did!"

Luke was off the desk in a flash and grabbing her tightly by the arms. "Don't ever compare me to him," he warned darkly.

"Then don't ever call me a liar!" she shot back, her eyes sparkling with temper. "I told you why I married him and it's the whole truth, whether you like it or not. I was never in love with him or remotely attracted to him!"

"Then why the hell did you marry him without even trying to get to the truth?"

"Until this morning, I thought I knew the whole ugly truth. How could any normal human being suspect such an evil scheme?" she asked, and then continued, "I panicked. I admit it. I made a stupid, hasty decision that I'll pay for the rest of my life. But at the time I didn't see any way to protect Butch or avoid Shane's blackmail attempts."

They were both breathing harshly, their chests rising and falling with exertion even though they didn't move an inch. Susan had never seen his eyes so dark and dangerous.

"Do you have any idea what it did to me to watch that film and know what you must have gone through to protect Butch?" he demanded roughly.

In the face of his anger, she didn't remind him of how tenuous their relationship had been back then. Their romance had still been so fragile, so pure and sweet she hadn't wanted to soil it with a confession on her brother's behalf.

"You could have come to me," he declared flatly. "I thought we had something special going," he continued, allowing her a tiny glimpse at his vulnerability. Then he released her, turned away and covered the emotion with anger.

"But you decided to let Shane get away with it all. You gave him the weapon he wanted. Now you expect me to believe you love me when you had so damned little faith in me back then?"

Susan had no argument or defense against the truth. She hadn't realized Shane would use their marriage as a weapon against Luke. It had been purely selfish of her not to tell him the truth as soon as she'd learned it. Having that pointed out to her made her physically ill.

He had every reason to hate and mistrust her, and he certainly had reason to worry about making her the mother of his children. As desperately as she wanted a child, she knew she was the worst possible role model. Her experience as a responsible guardian was woefully bad.

"If it's any consolation, I hate myself more than you could ever hate me," she admitted, dropping her eyes to where her trembling fingers worried her wedding band.

"I let everyone down—you, Butch, my parents. If there was a way to change the past I'd gladly do it. But I can't." And he wasn't likely to forgive her anytime soon.

Luke's expression was a reflection of bitter anger and frustration. When he spoke, his voice was harder than she'd ever heard it. "None of us can change what's already done. We'll just have to live with the consequences."

Susan dared a glance at his features. Was one of the consequences his inability to accept her love? Would he never be able to trust her as completely as she trusted him? Or worse, would the truth destroy any budding feelings he had for her? The physical desire? The marital commitment?

She had to know. "Do you want me to pack and leave?" she forced herself to ask.

He swung around, scowling fiercely. "What the hell do you mean?"

Sobs climbed from her chest, and Susan couldn't force another word past her tightly constricted throat. Her eyes searched his for direction. Was he giving up on their marriage?

"This doesn't change anything between you and me," he said when understanding dawned. "We married for better or worse, remember? I meant it when I said I'd never let you go."

Relief flooded over her. If he thought she wanted to leave him, he was badly mistaken. Despite his disgust, she wasn't ready to give up on their relationship. He might not want her love, but that wouldn't lessen it.

She desperately needed a chance to redeem herself. She needed to earn his love and trust, and maybe repair some of the damage to her own self-esteem in the process.

The knowledge of the long, hard battle ahead of them made her incredibly weary. Too much tension and too little sleep added an edge of unreality to the situation. She felt weepy and distraught.

Without another word, she turned and left the room.

He didn't follow.

Chapter Nine

🙟

The next few weeks passed in a haze of worry for Susan. Luke worked from daylight to dusk and sometimes around the clock. She spent nearly as much time with the mares until all the new foals were born.

When they managed to get to bed together, he pulled her into his arms but she knew the sex was more of a physical release for him than the pleasure it should be. He kept himself under such rigid control that she sometimes wondered why he bothered.

Gone were the hours of sensual exploration. Gone, to be replaced by very carefully controlled sex. His loving never left her body unsatisfied, yet her heart bled each time he took her into his arms.

It wasn't hard to keep her days filled with work and activity, but sleep never came easily, even when she was physically exhausted. She didn't want to suffer another collapse so she did her best to eat right and rest when possible.

She spent endless hours wondering what, if anything, she could do to earn his trust, to break through the barriers he'd erected around his heart. There weren't any easy answers, but she did come up with a plan to return the Hanchart land to the family without breaking the terms of Shane's will. She ran it past the family's lawyer and had him draw up the paperwork. Then she waited for any small improvement in Luke's attitude so that she could address the issue, but he remained unforgiving.

Susan tried her best to be patient. She never criticized him and made no demands. She kept telling herself it would get better, yet nothing seemed to get through to him. It was torture to be so close to him, close enough to reach out and touch him, yet know that he wouldn't welcome any overtures from her. His attitude didn't invite intimacy of any kind.

Sometimes she ached for kisses that expressed a deeper hunger than the physical. She longed to snuggle closer to his big, warm body, yet dared not make a move lest she invite another rejection. She walked on eggshells and slept restlessly at night, wondering how long she'd have to continue to pay for her past mistakes. How long was a long enough sentence for crimes of the heart? For not having enough faith in Luke when it had meant the most? How long would it take to renew his faith in her? In them? In their relationship?

Her nerves were frayed, and she found herself growing weepy at the slightest provocation. Luke lost weight and Rosa fussed over both of them. Neither ate properly and it was obvious they weren't sleeping well.

On one occasion John commented that they both looked like hell. They shrugged it off as part of the busy season on the ranch. That much was true. Since the firing of Rod Matthews they'd been shorthanded and it was a hard time of year to hire extra help.

To make matters worse, the work was hindered by more than the usual problems with livestock and equipment. Gates were unaccountably left open and equipment developed mechanical failures.

Before long it became evident that someone was trying to sabotage their efforts to keep the ranch running smoothly. Susan suspected that one or both of the Matthewses was responsible, but she never voiced her opinion. She didn't know if Luke had the same suspicions or what he planned to do about it.

She heard through Rosa that gossip was rampant in Monroe about a fight between Rod and his uncle. The senior Matthews was threatening to disinherit him if he didn't make some lifestyle changes.

Susan rarely left the ranch, so she never saw Rod and never heard the rumors herself. She was just relieved that something besides her marriage had captured the community's attention. She'd never enjoyed being the object of gossip, and her relationship with Luke was too fragile to subject to more criticism or ridicule.

A month passed before things started to slow down a little and Luke started spending more time at the house. Susan wondered if he was finally coming to terms with his initial anger and frustration. She hoped he was getting it all out of his system so they could give their marriage a real chance.

Then late one afternoon she was exercising Mariado when she heard gunshots. Luke and Juan were clearing a felled tree from a field on the east side of the property and the sounds originated from that direction. She wondered what type of trouble had erupted.

Gunshots weren't a totally foreign sound on a working ranch. They were sometimes troubled by predators after stock, but it was unusual for a weapon to be fired unless the staff was alerted to the cause beforehand.

Deciding to investigate, she turned Mariado in the direction of the field where they were working. It took her only a few minutes to reach the cluster of vehicles at the edge of the field, where she was waved to a halt by Juan.

"What's up?" she asked, calming Mariado as he approached.

His response was curt and rough with concern. "We've got a shooter."

Susan's eyes widened. "Someone shot at you while you were working?" she asked in amazement.

"It's a lone man with a high-powered rifle. He waited until I'd pulled the truck over here to unload and then pinned Luke down behind what's left of the tree."

For an instant, she couldn't draw air into her lungs. Fear lanced her, cutting deeply. The thought of Luke being in danger brought a rush of sick dread.

Her gaze flew across the open field. Several of their men had congregated in a small copse of trees, but the fallen tree was nearer the center of the field, a hundred or so yards from any other protection. Two sides were wide-open pasture, but a rocky ridge bordered the other two sides and formed an arc around Luke's location. He was effectively trapped.

"Someone's on the ridge?"

"Yeah. He's been taking shots at Luke, and he's slowly moving down the ridge to circle around where he can get a clean shot."

"You can't drive out there and get him?" she demanded, voice rising with anxiety.

"I tried, but he shot the windshield and one tire out of the truck. Luke told us to stay back. Wilcox wanted to ride out, but the shooter's too good to risk it."

"Luke's armed?"

"No. His rifle's in the truck."

Her heart sank. Without a weapon, he couldn't keep the shooter at bay. "What's his plan?"

Juan's expression tightened. "We called the sheriff and he's sending a helicopter. Luke doesn't want this guy to get away. A couple of our men are trying to circle around behind him on the ridge, but our best bet is the copter."

Another shot rang out and their attention shifted to the field. Bark flew from the tree trunk so close to Luke's head that her teeth clenched in fear.

Her tone was grim. "In the meantime, he's just going to stay out there like a sitting duck while this guy moves close enough to get a clean shot?"

"I don't like it either," Juan growled.

It didn't take her more than two seconds to formulate her own plan. The hell with catching the shooter. The sheriff could worry about him later. She wasn't leaving Luke unarmed in a field while someone tried to kill him.

She wouldn't lose him. She loved him too much to even consider the pain of losing him the way she'd lost the rest of her family. She couldn't let anything happen to him. Not if there was any way on Earth to protect him. "Get me Luke's rifle," she insisted tersely.

Juan's head shot back and he stared up at her in consternation. "What do you think you're going to do?"

"I'm taking it out to him. It could be another half an hour before the sheriff gets here."

"The hell!" Juan started to argue, but she threw up a hand to stop him.

Her tone and expression brooked no arguments.

"Mariado's so fast that I can cross the distance before that madman up there has time to readjust his sights. She's used to me and won't be spooked if I slide down her left side to stay out of range."

The foreman was grumbling and shaking his head. "Luke won't like it. He told me to stay back. He'll probably kill every last one of us for letting you take that kind of risk."

Susan knew that even though Juan wasn't pleased with her plan, he realized it could work. The men were too big a target. She and Mariado could do it. They were a team and her horse never balked at anything she asked of her.

Luke needed some protection. His life might depend on him being able to defend himself if the gunman got any closer.

"At least he'll still be around to lose his temper," she said, her expression grim and set.

Juan's hesitation was brief. Then he went to the truck for the rifle. He had the men shift so there was a clear path to

Luke. She'd need some space to get Mariado to a full gallop before she broke into the open pasture.

She waited impatiently for everyone to get prepared, patting Mariado's neck and praying the gunman wouldn't shoot her horse. She didn't think there was any chance, but it didn't matter when compared to Luke's safety. Nothing mattered when compared to him.

She pulled her feet out of the stirrups and shifted all her weight down the horse's left side, preparing Mariado for the ride. It would be difficult to cling to the side of the saddle and carry a rifle without the use of the stirrups, but she would need to make a swift dismount.

The horse was trained for calf roping, so she was used to quick starts and abrupt stops. Susan knew they could pull it off. Adrenaline began pumping through her veins as Juan handed her the rifle and she grasped it tightly under her left arm.

"Be careful," he demanded roughly.

She nodded. Another shot rang out and her fingers clenched around the reins. She wasn't going to let some idiot with a gun keep threatening Luke's life.

With a gentle tug of the reins and a nudge of her knees, she alerted the horse that they were ready to move again. Mariado, always ready to run, bunched her muscles and then headed toward the field like a shot at Susan's urging.

Within seconds they were at a full gallop and leaving the copse of trees for open field. Susan's heart raced too. She allowed the few seconds she imagined it would take the gunman to redirect his fire then slid to the horse's side.

The pounding of Mariado's hooves rivaled the pounding of her pulse as blood roared through her ears. Wind whipped her hair wildly and dust flew in her face, but she kept Luke in sight. He was swearing so loud she could hear him above all the ruckus, but all she was concerned about was reaching him with his weapon.

Another shot rang out, this time aimed at her. Susan heard the bullet ricochet off some part of the saddle and whiz past her right shoulder. Then she was urging Mariado to an abrupt halt and sliding into Luke's arms. He snatched her to safety behind the tree trunk, and then shouted to send the startled horse galloping back to cover.

His expression was tight as he grabbed the rifle and pushed Susan into the curve of the tree trunk where the upended roots offered more cover. She was breathing so hard she couldn't speak but he had no trouble verbalizing a string of raw curses.

His eyes were dark and furious as he flipped the safety off the rifle and shoved the clip into place. He took aim and fired several shots toward the ridge. The shooter returned fire, but now that Luke was armed he didn't dare move any closer.

It was a standoff, but a long and noisy one. Susan huddled closer to the tree and covered her ears with her hands until the worst of it was over and Luke finally stopped shooting. When she eventually lowered her hands it was to the sound of an approaching helicopter.

Relief washed over her. Help had arrived. The chopper passed over them toward the ridge, and then she heard the engines cut back. There was shouting from a distance as the sheriff used a bullhorn to demand the gunman throw down his weapon. She held her breath, hoping he'd comply without endangering anyone else.

"He's surrendering," Luke said, straightening from his crouched position. He laid his gun aside and turned toward her.

His eyes were turbulent when he focused on her. "Are you all right?" he growled, reaching out a hand to help her up.

Susan couldn't speak. She was trembling so violently that she didn't trust her voice. She quickly jerked her hand from his grasp and stepped aside so that he wouldn't realize how shaken she was.

His expression tightened even more, eyes blazing with fury. She didn't know if he was furious with her or just the whole situation. She averted her eyes so that he couldn't read the raw emotion she was too traumatized to hide. Before either of them could say anything they were surrounded by people. Everyone on the property had been alerted and they all wanted to make sure neither of them had been harmed.

Juan was the first to reach them, enveloping Susan in a bear hug. Then John was grabbing her for a hug while Luke began yelling at the men for letting her risk her life.

"What the hell's the matter with you?" he raged. "Have you all taken loss of your senses? That guy was good. He could have picked her off the horse if he'd reacted fast enough! His shots came too damned close as it was!"

Juan and the men didn't make excuses nor explain that the gunman's accuracy was exactly the reason they'd welcomed Susan's help.

"You knew the sheriff was on the way! Why the hell didn't you just follow my orders and keep everybody back?"

Susan realized that he needed to vent his anger, yet the tone of his voice made her tremble even more. Reaction to the scare she'd received began to set in and she clung tightly to John for another long minute.

"Can you get Susan up to the house while I deal with the sheriff?" Luke asked his grandfather, his tone losing some of its heat. "I'll be up as soon as I can."

John agreed and steered her toward his pickup truck at the edge of the meadow. Susan walked to the truck on shaky legs, relieved to take a seat in the cab.

The sheriff's helicopter landed in the open pasture and they watched as Luke and the men went out to meet him. Then John drove her to the house without another word. She thanked him and let Rosa fuss over her some more but soon pleaded the need for rest and headed for the master bedroom.

* * * * *

A short time later Susan heard Luke climbing the stairs, and she lifted a hand to swipe the tears from her face. She braced herself for more of his anger but continued to pack her clothes in a couple of ragged suitcases leftover from her college days.

The door swung open behind her but she didn't turn to face him. He stepped inside and quietly closed the door.

Suddenly the whole room was charged with explosive tension.

"What the hell's going on?" he demanded in a low growl.

She cleared her throat of tears, determined to get through the next few minutes without breaking down and crying like a baby. Keeping her back to him, she offered an explanation.

"I think it's time that I leave. It's obvious that we're never going to make this marriage work, so we might as well cut our losses right now."

He started to speak, but she interrupted him. "I've found a way to protect the Hanchart land other than securing it with our marriage," she explained, reaching into the drawer of the nightstand and retrieving a legal-sized envelope.

She turned briefly to give it to him, hand out but eyes downcast. When he didn't take it she laid it on top of the stand instead.

"I've decided to deed the land to your firstborn child," she said, swallowing more tears. "That way the land can remain in the family without me actually selling it to you and without breaking the terms of Shane's will.

"I had the papers drawn up to make you guardian of the property until your son or daughter reaches an age that you consider responsible enough to take possession."

The idea had come to her one night after they'd made love, when she'd thought about the possibility of being pregnant with Luke's child. At the time she'd imagined herself the mother of that child.

Even though she loved him with all her heart, the day's events had convinced her that he was never going to return those feelings. He was never going to consider her an equal partner in their marriage. He even resented her help when his life was in danger.

Sometime during those traumatic minutes out there in the pasture, she'd realized that she couldn't go on living a lie. It was just too hard to love him so desperately and feel him growing more distant each day. Before long his resentment would grow into hatred and she couldn't bear the thought.

Now was the time to make a clean break and allow them both to get on with their lives. A sob caught at her throat but she fought for control. She folded and refolded clothing, waiting for him to agree with her and leave her alone again.

His voice, when he finally spoke, was so low and deep that she had to strain to hear it. "Did you lie when you said you loved me?"

Susan's hand flew to cover her mouth and stifle an unexpected sob. He certainly knew how to cut her to the quick. She might not be the woman of his dreams but she wasn't a liar.

"No."

"Did you lie when you said you wanted a real marriage, a family and a lifetime commitment?"

The questions didn't get any easier. "No."

"Have you changed your mind about all those things? Realized you don't really love me?"

Her love for him had changed, had gotten more intense, more passionate and more heartbreaking in depth.

"No." Her response was a thready whisper.

Then Luke touched her. It was little more than a hesitant touch of his fingers to her back but it was her undoing. They were always more honest and open with their physical contact than with the verbal.

She turned and Luke swiftly enveloped her in his arms, dragging her close to his chest and hugging her tightly. She wrapped her arms around his waist.

"I was so frightened for you out there," she mumbled against his shirt. He was hard and warm and vitally healthy. She clung tighter, trying to absorb the scent and feel of him.

She heard a groan rumble from chest and he clutched the back of her head. "You couldn't have been half as scared as I was when I saw you riding across that field with no protection at all."

Luke scared? The very idea made Susan's breath catch. She tilted her head back so that she could see his face. He returned her steady regard without flinching or attempting to hide the raw emotion displayed there,

What she saw in his eyes made her heart stop then begin to race. Could all that emotion be directed at her alone? "You were frightened for me?"

Luke moaned, closing his eyes and hugging her more tightly. He sank his fingers into her hair and held her head against his heart. Then he lowered his head until he was whispering in her ear.

"I've never been so scared in my life, and I never want to be again. I don't want you taking risks like that for me."

"I thought you were furious because I interfered and ignored your orders to stay out of the way."

"I was furious because I was scared," he admitted huskily, nuzzling her ear and neck with his face. "The thought of anything happening to you scared me a whole lot more than having a gun aimed at me."

Her heart soared. Did she dare believe that she was important to him? That he was beginning to care for her the way she cared for him? The thought brought new hope for their marriage. Maybe he was willing to give their relationship a chance to grow.

She had to know. It was hard to verbalize the next question but being held securely in his arms gave her courage. She pulled back until she could look him in the eyes again.

"Does that mean you're finally willing to forgive me and maybe learning to care about me a little?" she asked softly. "For more than a way to retain the Hanchart land? For more than a bed partner?"

Their gazes tangled, each searching the other's for a promise of true commitment.

"That means I love you more every day," he managed in a voice rough with emotion.

"Oh, Luke," she cried, her heart leaping with joy. She grasped his face in her hands and pulled him close for a kiss. Then their mouths locked, lips hard and demanding while their tongues danced to an ancient rhythm of love.

They were both breathless when their lips finally parted. "I love you so much!" she cried.

Luke laid his forehead against hers. "Dear God, I don't know what I ever did to deserve your love, but I'm selfish enough to want to keep it forever."

"You don't have any choice," she murmured. "You're stuck with it and me."

"You were going to leave me."

"Only because I so desperately needed your love," she explained softly. "I thought you were growing to hate me. I couldn't bear that, Luke. I had decided I couldn't stay if you didn't really want me."

"I want you," he insisted hoarsely. "Every minute of every day for the rest of our lives. Can you promise me that?"

"I can promise you'll always have my love no matter what the future holds. Nothing is going to change that."

"Nothing?"

"Nothing."

"Promise?"

"Promise."

"Sealed with a kiss?" he teased, capturing her mouth with his again and wrapping her securely in his arms.

* * * * *

Hours later, when dinner was over and everyone had left the house for the night, Luke and Susan finally found themselves alone in the family room.

She'd showered and slipped on worn cutoff jeans with a white tank top. Her bare feet were curled beneath her on the sofa. Luke had on clean but faded jeans that rode low on his hips. He'd showered too, and pulled on a soft blue T-shirt that was equally formfitting. Just looking at him made her pulse accelerate. Every time she thought of somebody trying to kill him, she felt ill.

"It's over," he insisted, watching her from the opposite side of the room. "Don't let it worry you anymore."

Susan lowered her lashes. It was disconcerting to have him reading her mind and witnessing her vulnerability. She couldn't help being upset every time she thought of the events of the afternoon.

"I can't believe Rod Matthews was stupid enough to try to kill you. I've never liked him but I never thought he was capable of cold-blooded murder. You don't kill someone for firing you."

"That was only part of it," Luke explained. "I let him know I suspected him of conspiring with Shane on that crime spree. I'd warned him about the drinking and drugs, but he didn't listen. He blamed me for all his problems."

Susan shook her head in disbelief. She hoped they kept Rod locked up for a very long time, and she hoped she never had to reexperience the fear she'd felt when Luke's life was in danger.

"I'm just thankful nobody got hurt," she said.

Luke's eyes darkened and his voice went low as he moved closer. "I'm thankful I have a wife who's as brave as she is beautiful."

Her heart skipped a beat and her gaze locked with his. The warmth and admiration in his eyes filled her with joy.

"I'm not brave or beautiful."

Luke sat down beside her, scooping her into his lap. "You're everything a man could want."

She searched his face, wanting to believe, but so afraid. "Do you really think that?"

"Really," he whispered, caressing her cheek with his thumb. "I've never been very good at expressing myself, but I want you to know how special I think you are."

"You're not just saying that?"

Luke shifted her slightly so that he could reach into his pocket. He pulled out a small jewelry box and snapped the lid. She gasped at the beauty of the diamond solitaire tucked into red velvet folds.

His smile was tight, his tone tightly controlled. "Do you like it?" he asked.

She sensed a wealth of insecurity in the question.

"It's gorgeous," she whispered, reaching out to touch the brilliant gem.

"Try it on," he insisted.

Susan slipped the ring from the box and slid it next to her wedding band. It was perfect.

He'd asked her preference about a wedding band before buying one, but never mentioned a diamond. "Did you get it with our rings?" she asked, wondering why he hadn't given it to her after the ceremony.

He hesitated briefly, his eyes searching hers. "I bought it three years ago."

The admission halted her breathing and then brought a rush of emotions. Guilt and regret warred with warmth and jubilation.

"You were going to ask me to marry you?" she asked softly. It was sad to realize what a horrible mistake she'd made back then, but she couldn't change the past.

"Yeah."

Her eyes searched his. She remembered Caroline's suggestion that John was behind any marriage proposal.

"Why?" she asked, holding her breath.

Luke grasped her hand and drew it to his mouth for a kiss. He brushed his lips over the rings.

His voice was little more a rough whisper. "Because I fell in love with you. I had to fight those feelings while you were married to Shane. It was hard to get past my ravaged pride and the gut-deep anger, but I never stopped loving you."

The simple words were backed up by the adoration in his eyes and sincerity in his tone. For an instant it was all Susan could do to push air in and out of her lungs. She wanted to bask in the warmth of his eyes.

"Not just because of what happened today? Not just because you want a family or for any other reason except you love just me?"

"Just everything about you."

"Promise?"

Luke gave her a lopsided grin. "Promise."

"Forever?" she demanded.

"Forever."

"Oh, Luke!"

Then she was locking her arms around his neck and dragging him close for a kiss. Several minutes later, he pulled his mouth from hers.

"Say the words to me," he insisted.

Susan was high on life and decided to tease him. "You told me not to say them again."

He groaned. "I changed my mind."

"I don't know," she paused for effect. "I don't want to do anything that would upset you."

Another groan rumbled from his chest. "You want me to beg?" he asked, eyes sparkling with challenge.

She pretended to consider the idea. Then his tongue touched her lips in a gentle, provocative little lick. She moaned and acquiesced.

"I love you, love you, love you," she chanted, giving him hard, hungry little kisses to accent the words.

Why an electronic book?

We live in the Information Age—an exciting time in the history of human civilization, in which technology rules supreme and continues to progress in leaps and bounds every minute of every day. For a multitude of reasons, more and more avid literary fans are opting to purchase e-books instead of paper books. The question from those not yet initiated into the world of electronic reading is simply: *Why?*

1. *Price.* An electronic title at Ellora's Cave Publishing and Cerridwen Press runs anywhere from 40% to 75% less than the cover price of the exact same title in paperback format. Why? Basic mathematics and cost. It is less expensive to publish an e-book (no paper and printing, no warehousing and shipping) than it is to publish a paperback, so the savings are passed along to the consumer.

2. *Space.* Running out of room in your house for your books? That is one worry you will never have with electronic books. For a low one-time cost, you can purchase a handheld device specifically designed for e-reading. Many e-readers have large, convenient screens for viewing. Better yet, hundreds of titles can be stored within your new library—on a single microchip. There are a variety of e-readers from different manufacturers. You can also read e-books on your PC or laptop computer. (Please note that

Ellora's Cave does not endorse any specific brands. You can check our websites at www.ellorascave.com or www.cerridwenpress.com for information we make available to new consumers.)

3. *Mobility.* Because your new e-library consists of only a microchip within a small, easily transportable e-reader, your entire cache of books can be taken with you wherever you go.

4. *Personal Viewing Preferences.* Are the words you are currently reading too small? Too large? Too... ANNOYING? Paperback books cannot be modified according to personal preferences, but e-books can.

5. *Instant Gratification.* Is it the middle of the night and all the bookstores near you are closed? Are you tired of waiting days, sometimes weeks, for bookstores to ship the novels you bought? Ellora's Cave Publishing sells instantaneous downloads twenty-four hours a day, seven days a week, every day of the year. Our webstore is never closed. Our e-book delivery system is 100% automated, meaning your order is filled as soon as you pay for it.

Those are a few of the top reasons why electronic books are replacing paperbacks for many avid readers.

As always, Ellora's Cave and Cerridwen Press welcome your questions and comments. We invite you to email us at Comments@ellorascave.com or write to us directly at Ellora's Cave Publishing Inc., 1056 Home Avenue, Akron, OH 44310-3502.

CERRÍDWEN PRESS

Cerridwen, the Celtic goddess of wisdom, was the muse who brought inspiration to storytellers and those in the creative arts.

Cerridwen Press encompasses the best and most innovative stories in all genres of today's fiction.

Visit our website and discover the newest titles by talented authors who still get inspired — much like the ancient storytellers did...

once upon a time.

www.cerridwenpress.com